Struker stood, hand pressed to the bleeding gash on his cheek, facing the solitary monk. "You may be good," he said, as he drew from his holster a Luger pistol. "But you're not bulletproof." He aimed the pistol point-blank at his enemy and pulled the trigger four times.

The monk flipped, then dove and rolled, eluding the first three bullets; for the fourth, the Tibetan snatched up an iron cook-plate and blocked it with a resounding *ping*. Struker swore silently to himself and fired again.

This time, the bullet found its mark: the monk shuddered slightly, then stared down at the bleeding wound in his side in utter amazement. He took several staggering steps backward . . . then dropped completely from Struker's line of vision.

When at last—gasping and perspiring, despite the cold—Struker reached the bottom of the cliff, he turned away from it and trudged over the uneven terrain to the spot where he had seen his foe lying. . . .

But the monk was not there.

BULLETPROOF MONK

J.M. DILLARD

BASED ON THE MOVIE *BULLETPROOF MONK*
WRITTEN BY ETHAN REIFF & CYRUS VORIS

POCKET **STAR** BOOKS
New York   London   Toronto   Sydney   Singapore

This book is a work of fiction. Names, characters, places and incidents are products of the author's imagination or are used fictitiously. Any resemblance to actual events or locales or persons, living or dead, is entirely coincidental.

Due to production and time constraints, some parts of this novelization may differ from the final cut of the film.

An *Original* Publication of POCKET BOOKS

A Pocket Star Book published by
POCKET BOOKS, a division of Simon & Schuster, Inc.
1230 Avenue of the Americas, New York, NY 10020

ISBN: 0-7434-7431-7

First Pocket Books printing April 2003

10 9 8 7 6 5 4 3 2 1

POCKET STAR BOOKS and colophon are registered
trademarks of Simon & Schuster, Inc.

For information regarding special discounts for bulk purchases,
please contact Simon & Schuster Special Sales at 1-800-456-6798
or business@simonandschuster.com

Printed in the U.S.A.

Om ah hum vajra guru padma siddhi hum.
—The Vajra Guru mantra

May all beings be well and happy! May all beings find freedom and joy!
—A Buddhist blessing

TIBET
1943

Prologue

Years before, he had begun actively to forget his own name—the name given him by his mother, now, too, no more than a ghostly memory. If he thought of himself—and his Buddhist practice demanded that he do so as little as possible, for Self was no more than illusion—it was as Brother Monk, one of many brothers at the monastery perched atop the Roof of the World, among the Himalayan Mountains, blinding white and regal against the piercing blue sky, ascending higher than the clouds.

At this particular time—Time itself being an illusion like Self, nothing more than a series of changes to the external world, a reminder of the impermanence of all things—Brother Monk had quite entirely forgotten himself. Balanced precariously on an aged wood plank and rope bridge strung above a fathomless chasm between two mountains, his well-trained body tensed for the next strike from his opponent, a man who had also reached full maturity, who also wore the saffron robes of a Tibetan monk.

The opponent struck out, forearms slicing the air like well-honed blades, aiming for Brother Monk's head, neck, chest: there was no point in trying to focus on each blow, for it came too fast for the eye to see. Instead, Brother Monk opened all his faculties and *sensed* the coming attack, repelling it flawlessly, with equally blinding swiftness, blocking arm with arm, hand with hand.

And in the midst of the battle, his mind—after years of meditation, calm and undisturbed as a lake shining quicksilver in the sun—noted the tiniest movement beside him. On the nearby rope—thrashing furiously from the fighters' shifting weight—a cocoon smaller than his finger split open, and from it a butterfly, wings damp and clinging to its body, emerged.

Brother Monk did not let himself be distracted from answering his enemy's every move with one of his own. But with his peripheral vision, he watched and appreciated the vision of the butterfly as it unfurled its wings, delicate and jewel-like, to the Himalayan sun. In the thin atmosphere, the dazzling sun dried them instantly, and the shimmering creature took flight.

Brother Monk's mind was uncluttered enough to realize that coincidence was but another illusion; purpose and meaning abounded everywhere, if one learned only to see beyond samsara, this apparent reality which was not the true, unchanging Real. He knew the butterfly was a sign: a symbol of rebirth, of enlightenment, of achieving one's ultimate purpose. He prayed only that he was ready, and worthy.

At once, his opponent, bland-faced, eyes utterly serene, managed to land a blow upon Brother Monk's shoulder—making Brother realize that he had focused, if only for an instant, on himself, a path that always led to defeat. One foot slipped on the plank beneath him, and he clung desperately to the rope that the butterfly had just deserted.

Just as swiftly, he cleared his mind, regained his balance, and answered the blow, fiercely.

His enemy evaded his attack and in answer began to kick the age-silvered planks from the bridge into Brother's face—launching a series of deadly wooden projectiles, each of which had borne for centuries the weight of monks' feet.

Brother Monk had no choice but to take the defensive. Sensing, not seeing, he struck first one plank, then the next, and the next, all with lightning speed, averting them. They sailed first upward, then down to their final resting place—the deep chasm below, darkened by the shadows of the mountains.

The attack continued until at last the two combatants faced each other, breathing heavily, balanced atop two bare lengths of rope, and no more: the last plank now rested fathoms beneath them, in the shadows.

For a heartbeat, Brother Monk and his opponent regarded each other in silence.

Who first moved, he could not have said; the action of both men seemed to him simultaneous. Brother Monk launched himself into the air, feet first, flying at his enemy. At the same instant, he saw his enemy likewise come sailing toward him.

The collision would have sent them both plummeting down into the chasm.

Instinctively, Brother Monk undulated serpentine in midair, twisting away from his opponent. His body arced upward for an instant; when it came down, he immediately seized the ropes and regained his balance.

His attacker, however, went sailing down.

"Rinpoche!" Brother Monk cried out in horror to his opponent. "Master!"

He shot forth a hand and seized his beloved *rinpoche's*, his master's, foot.

Still dangling upside down over the ominous drop, yet as perfectly at ease as if he had been sitting over a cup of steaming tea, the Master smiled benevolently up at him.

"Good catch," the Master said lightly. "Your training is complete."

Brother Monk stood in an attitude of humble reverence as his master raised a prayer flag, bright yellow for spirit, atop a high pole. He watched as the wind caught hold of the flag and whipped it tautly, echoing the prayer upon it in his own mind:

Om ah hum vajra guru padma siddhi hum. . . .

The words were Sanskrit, but even in his mind, he pronounced them with a Tibetan accent, as he had been taught by his master: *Omya hung benza guru peme siddhi hung. . . .*

Oh, Vajra Guru, may you bring us both ordinary and supreme blessings and attainment. . . .

This was the mantra of the Vajra Guru, the one also called Padmasambhava, meaning the Lotus-Born, for it was said that he was born on a lotus blossom. Padmasambhava had brought the teachings of the Buddha to Tibet millennia before, and as such, he was revered as its Most Beloved Master, *Guru Rinpoche.*

His real name had been long ago forgotten.

Of all prayers, the Vajra Guru mantra was the most powerful, bringing with it *siddhis*, or magical abilities and blessings, in order to achieve enlightenment. The prayer was never uttered lightly in hopes of attaining something as foolish as external powers or wealth, or even to relieve one's physical suffering or difficulties in the world of samsara. It was to be used only for the holiest purpose: to free one's mind from grasping, to move toward liberation of the spirit, and to assist others in doing the same.

"This prayer flag symbolizes the ending of my destiny," the Master said, watching it flap for an instant in the strong wind; and then he looked down and smiled his serene smile at his protégé. "And the beginning of yours."

Brother Monk felt a wave of humility, then dismissed it as merely another form of self-involvement. It mattered not that he, among all in the *Sangha*, the community of believers, had been chosen to replace the Master; it was merely his karma, but his heart, his mind, was no different from his fellow monks', no worthier of compassion. He sensed them behind him, as they sat—a mere fifteen of them, though in earlier centuries, the monastery had been crowded—in lotus position on the ground before the temple, and he knew that each of them was silently repeating the prayer inscribed on the flag, invoking Padmasambhava.

Om ah hum vajra guru padma siddhi hum.

The monastery was utterly silent, save for the sound of the Master's voice, the flapping of the prayer flag, and the occasional chatter of the monkeys who milled about, searching for food scraps.

As Brother Monk watched, his mind empty, a brilliantly colored butterfly flitted about the prayer flag, then slowly sailed downward and lit atop the Master's shaved head. Brother Monk's studies of mental concentration permitted him to recognize the precise coloration on the wings, and to know that this was the same creature that had emerged from its cocoon while he and the Master had been fighting on the rope bridge.

The Master's dark eyes warmed at the sensation on his scalp; he raised a hand and gently prodded the butterfly onto a finger, then lowered it so that he might admire its beauty. As he watched it, he told the man standing before him:

"When you first came to me you were the most undisciplined youth I had ever laid eyes on." He gestured at the monks sitting in front of the temple. "I could hardly believe what my brother monks said—that you had fulfilled the three noble prophecies." He drew in a breath before listing them. "You had 'defeated an army of enemies while a flock of cranes circled above,' you had 'battled for love in a palace of jade,' and you had 'led the brothers you never knew to the family you never had.'" He paused, then lifted the butterfly to his lips and blew gently on its back. It fluttered its wings, slowly at first, then more swiftly, and at last flew away.

The Master glanced up and met his protégé's gaze directly. "Now you must make the final sacrifice by casting off the last worldly possession that remains to weigh you down. You must give up . . . your *name*."

Brother Monk fell to the cold earth and prostrated himself at his master's feet, nodding his shaven head. "I've already forgotten it, Master."

The Master led him inside the Temple of Sublime Truth, a structure as ancient as Buddhism's arrival in Tibet. Windowless, its walls hewn from dark wood, the temple was shrouded in perpetual gloom, eased only by the rows of flickering butterlamps and candles set upon the shelves of a simple shrine. The lamps signified the illumination that burns away the darkness of ignorance; in their center rested a statue the size of a man's arm from fingertip to elbow, rendered of gleaming gold. This was Avalokiteshvara, the Buddha of Compassion, whose mantra was *om mane padme hum*. If Padmasambhava, the Vajra Guru, was the mind of Tibet, then surely Avalokiteshvara was its heart: he could be called upon to pour out the blessings of compassion on any situation, giving freely, using love to transform evil intent to good, purifying hearts; and it was he who led the recently dead safely to the realm of the buddhas.

On the shelf below the Buddha of Compassion were small golden bowls filled with clear water, symbolizing the clarity of mind that came with meditation and right thought; on the shelf above sat a humble-looking bamboo case. It was the case that at once caught Brother Monk's gaze as he stepped inside the temple, behind his master. So focused was he on what was to come that he did not notice the youngest monk—Brother Sogyal, a lad, still a good five winters away from being a man—duck into the temple behind him.

But the Master noticed all. He turned, blocking the boy, and in a voice infinitely firm yet still filled with good humor, said, "Not so fast, little one. Your big eyes have already seen enough for one day."

Brother Monk smiled inwardly. Sogyal was as sincere a monk as any, but his youthful curiosity often got the better of his desire to be obedient. During his final competition with his master, Brother Monk had had the suspicion that a third pair of eyes had been watching the entire spectacle: Sogyal's, from one of his many hiding places. And now the Master's comment confirmed that suspicion.

The blush on Sogyal's cheeks did the same. The boy quickly bowed to the Master, then shot a slightly envious look up at Brother Monk.

Brother Monk fixed a hard, impenetrable gaze on the lad . . . then softened it with a wink.

Sogyal scurried out the door—to another hiding place, no doubt, where he could see what was about to pass between Brother and the Master.

Brother Monk let go of any thought of Sogyal and instead regarded the ancient mural painted on one of the temple walls, from the minerals found in the mountains, in shades of crimson, saffron, gold, deep blues and greens. The image itself was terrifying: he felt the effects of fear in his own body at the sight, and breathed deeply until they passed.

The mural showed men, women, and children, all violently attacked by the four elements of air, fire, water, and earth. Brother knew it represented the utter destruction of all civilization by violent storms, flames, floods, and earthquakes. If the power of the four elements ever fell into grasping hands, hands whose heart was not filled with compassion for humankind, such would certainly be the result. . . .

Master Monk spoke next to him. "The nightmare of this picture is the reality against which our brotherhood has stood guard through the centuries. . . ." He reverently lifted the bamboo case from the shelf, opened it, and withdrew from it a delicate, age-weathered rice-paper scroll. "The Scroll of the Ultimate," he said, and for the first time since Brother Monk had come to the monastery, he saw the good humor fade from his master's eyes, saw a shadow creep into them. "If its words are spoken aloud, they have the power to turn this world into a paradise . . . or destroy it completely."

Impossibly, the air in the temple began to stir in a circular fashion, slowly at first, then faster; Brother Monk felt a tingling in his body, as if the wind contained unspent lightning. As odd as the occurrence was, he felt no fear: he knew he had been destined for this moment.

The Master faced him. In the Master's eyes, Brother saw the compassion and enlightenment of the Buddha, the wisdom-mind of Padmasambhava. In his heart, he knew that the knowledge he was about to receive had been passed on from master to student for thousands of years, from Padmasambhava on. And in Brother's eyes, his master was no less than the Buddha himself.

The wind swirled, so strong that had Brother tried to drop to the floor, he would have been held upright.

The Master spoke, his voice strong, ageless.

"Five times the Year of the Ram has passed since I became the Next for my honored predecessor . . . and his master before him and so on and so on. Now it is *your* turn."

The once-gloomy temple blazed with sudden light as the air itself became filled with brilliant, shimmering energy.

Bathed in light, blinded by it, Brother Monk saw nothing else, but felt the Master's powerful grip as he seized his student's forearms and held them tightly.

Brother's body shuddered slightly as it filled with a power so sacred, so intense that the doors to the Temple of Sublime Truth were blown open.

Young Brother Sogyal, huddled out of sight down in his hiding place in the temple, was not the only one to gasp aloud at the miraculous sight. Several hundred meters away, hidden behind an outcropping of rock, crouched a second watcher, this one blond and pale-skinned, with eyes the color of the thin Himalayan sky. His name was Struker, and he held the rank of colonel in the Nazi SS.

A thrill passed through Struker's own body as he watched the blinding surge of supernatural energy pass from the master monk's form into that of the student.

"Mein Gott," Struker whispered, though he most certainly did not believe in God. He did, however, believe in power; and now that belief—nurtured by

many years of research—that the Tibetans possessed it was confirmed.

It remained now only to take it from them.

Before Brother Monk's eyes, the shimmering brilliance evaporated, leaving the Temple of Sublime Truth once again in gloom. As for himself, he felt little changed . . . physically. Mentally, however, his mind was filled with a peace, a clarity he had never before experienced.

But even the shadows in the temple could not hide the metamorphosis undergone by his master. The beloved teacher's skin had shriveled, his eyes turned sunken, his black hair white; even his shoulders sagged with extreme age.

"It is done," the Master said, his voice now cracked, reedy. In a matter of seconds, he had aged more than half a century. He passed the scroll to his student, who took it reverently, with hands that trembled of their own accord, despite his attempts to control them.

Brother Monk was Brother Monk no more. . . . Now he indeed had no name. From henceforth, he thought of himself merely as the monk—no more, no less.

Now wizened and stooped, the Master led him to the open door of the temple. They were equals now, and the Master spoke to him as such, but always with the good humor that marked the enlightened.

"It's finally time for me to do what I've wanted to do since those pesky British showed up in 1904."

The monk looked up at him curiously. "What is that, Master?"

The old man smiled. "Take a vacation."

As the two Tibetans stood perfectly profiled in the temple doorway, Colonel Struker lowered his binoculars and reached for the radio transmitter beside him. His heart was hammering—this was, after all, a moment he had long dreamed of, one he had scarcely dared hope would ever come to pass. Yet he had believed in it strongly enough to convince the Führer to allow him to bring a secret contingent of SS Kommandos to this near-inaccessible place.

But despite his physical reaction of excitement, Struker's mind remained deadly cold and focused on the task to be accomplished. He spoke into the transmitter, his voice flat, toneless, ruthless.

"Now."

And as the monk with no name watched in horror, a burst of machine-gun fire tore into his beloved master's body; the saffron robes, reduced to shreds in the old man's midsection, turned an immediate, alarming scarlet.

The teacher fell into his student's arms. As bullets continued to rake the temple's interior and the brothers outside dove for cover, the monk set his master gently on the floor, then hurried to shut the door—just before a fleeing monkey scurried inside.

The monk knelt at the Master's side.

"Protect . . . the scroll . . ." the old man whispered, then let go a hitching breath; at its end, his eyes, always so bright, dulled.

The monk did not permit himself to weep, though that was his natural human reaction, born out of his affection for the Master's human form. Instead, he reminded himself sternly that this was rather a cause for rejoicing: for his master had been enlightened, and had no doubt attained the *dharmakaya*, the supreme achievement, freedom from the Wheel of Birth and Rebirth. If he chose, the Master could reside in nirvana in bliss with the other blessed ones who had achieved buddhahood. . . .

More likely, he would choose, as many buddhas did, to incarnate and return to the earthly realm to help others on the path to enlightenment.

Gently, the monk closed his teacher's unseeing eyes. "Enjoy your vacation, Master."

There came a subtle stirring of cloth. The monk whirled, noted the monkey who had run inside, then caught sight of something more: poor young Brother Sogyal, trembling violently in his hiding place in a dark corner of the temple.

The monk addressed him in a tone that brooked no argument. "Stay hidden—no matter what."

Outside, the gunfire ceased. Struker watched as eight of his SS Kommandos emerged from their hiding places and converged on the temple.

As they did, the community of monks rose from

the ground and stood elbow-to-elbow, forming a human chain that blocked entry to the temple.

The Kommandos waited until Struker came forth from his lookout behind the outcropping of rock. The colonel marched into the monastery courtyard, trying hard to surpress his glee at the Tibetan paraphernalia surrounding him: malas, or prayer beads, wooden bowls, the ocher-feathered "wisdom crowns" worn in certain ceremonies, musical instruments. . . . These were things he had seen only crude drawings of, or read third-hand descriptions of. . . . Now all these things that he had spent his life studying were here before him to admire.

His first impulse was to order his men to fire; but his pleasure at the moment was so great he felt an uncharacteristic desire to be generous. He stepped up to the closest monk—a typical Tibetan, skin a light, weathered brown, cheekbones high and pronounced, eyes shining black and deep-set—and bowed to him, a typical Tibetan greeting, then performed the first few steps of a traditional folk dance.

"My brother monks!" he addressed them, smiling. "You have seen the destructive power which is mine to command . . . but this is not my only power. I also have the power . . . to leave this blessed monastery—in peace." He paused, and studied the faces surrounding him, all perfectly composed, all expressionless, impossible to read. "No doubt you are wondering why I call you my 'brothers.' You see, back in Germany, the Führer's top researchers tell us our Aryan blood originated somewhere in Asia—maybe Persia, maybe India . . . maybe right here in Tibet." His smile turned dark. "So I trust you will do what's best for our family . . . and step aside."

In response, the monks stared back at him in defiant silence; one monk began to pray, then the others took up the chant. It was an eerie sound, a combination of several octaves that sounded more like a force of nature than human voices; it was a sound Struker had never heard before, and it chilled him to the bone.

The fact that it frightened him also infuriated him. The smile faded from his face, replaced by an expression far grimmer.

Though he had never heard monks' voices raised in a chant before, he recognized the prayer: it was the Vajra Guru mantra—*om ah hum vajra guru padma siddhi hum*—though the pronunciation seemed quite odd, certainly not proper Sanskrit.

Very well, let them pray to the Guru for protection and blessings. Let them see what good their little prayer would do them against the power of SS Kommandos' MP-41 machine pistols.

Struker shrugged, then turned his back on the monks, and signaled curtly to his men to fire.

Inside the closed Temple of Sublime Truth, the nameless monk shut his eyes at the deafening volley of machine-gun fire. His first instinct was to feel horror; his second, to pray silently to the blessed buddha Avalokiteshvara to lead his dead brothers safely to the land of the dead, by recalling the buddha's mantra.

Om mane padme hum . . .

Outside, Struker studied the work of his Kommandos with pleasure: the Tibetan monks, their robes now bloodied tatters, lay lifeless on the ground, some corpses resting atop others. Dark crimson stains fanned out on the earth beneath some of the bodies, creating gruesome silhouettes.

The fools—did they really believe their mantras and prayer beads could protect them from the power of Nazi bullets? Struker was mollified to find all trace of defiance gone from their eyes and expressions now; death left behind stark blankness.

He caught his men's attention and gestured toward the temple. "The scroll."

He nodded at two of the Kommandos, who moved cautiously toward the closed doors of the temple.

Unconcerned—nothing, after all, could still be alive in there—Struker let his eye be caught by a flash of color. On a nearby flower, a butterfly had landed, one more brilliantly colorful than any he had seen in his native Germany. Mildly intrigued, he reached a hand down and plucked the insect up in his fingers and studied it for an instant.

His habit with bugs, once he lost interest in them, was to crush them—but before he could harm this one, the sound of automatic weapons fire distracted him. From inside the temple came a few short bursts, followed by silence. . . .

Struker released the butterfly, which flew off at once. And at the realization that the scroll he had so long sought was mere seconds from being in his grasp, he smiled.

Abruptly, the two SS soldiers were hurled from the temple and landed, unconscious, near Struker's feet. An instant later, the pieces of their MP-41 machine pistols followed.

Apparently, many more monks were hiding inside and had found a way to protect themselves from the gunfire—but they would not last long against a cadre of trained SS men. Struker felt a rush of heat to his face, and a fury laced with hatred. These foreigners might fancy themselves enlightened; perhaps they were even the forebears of the Aryan race . . . but they were still foreigners, and would be made to bow, like the rest of the world, to German might.

Rage smoldering in his eyes, he looked at his men.

"We all go in—*together*."

Motioning for his men to follow, he took a step toward the temple door . . .

And was immediately attacked by a chattering blur of fur, teeth, and claws that slashed out at his face.

Struker screamed at the sudden pain, for an instant too terrified to realize his assailant was only a monkey.

In the meantime, he was distantly aware that a lone Tibetan monk had emerged from the temple, and was now unleashing a series of kicks and punches on his men—who had been distracted by the monkey, and were now too disoriented by their new attacker to shoot them. For Struker, it happened far too fast: in less time than it had taken his soldiers to execute the monks, this single Tibetan had, with only his hands and feet, disabled his entire squad of men.

At last, Struker stood, hand pressed to the bleeding gash on his cheek, facing the solitary monk. A cold, hard wind began to blow, causing the prayer flag above them to snap loudly.

Over the monk's shoulder was slung a bamboo case, and in that case, its outline visible, was the scroll, the one thing on earth for which Struker would risk his life.

Struker glared at the monk with unalloyed hate. "You may be good," he said, as he drew from his holster a Luger pistol. "But you're not bulletproof." He aimed the pistol point-blank at his enemy and pulled the trigger four times.

Struker watched with disbelief as the monk flipped, then dove and rolled, eluding the first three bullets; for the fourth, the Tibetan snatched up an iron cook-plate and blocked it with a resounding *ping*.

Struker swore silently to himself and fired again.

This time, the bullet found its mark: the monk shuddered slightly, then stared down at the bleeding wound in his side in utter amazement. He took several staggering steps backward . . . then dropped completely from Struker's line of vision.

Struker ran after him—then, with a lurch and gasp, stopped abruptly in his tracks, waving his arms to maintain balance.

He stood on the edge of a sheer cliff: at the bottom of the drop, some three hundred meters below, the Tibetan lay motionless on the rocks.

The German retreated from the edge and hurriedly removed his backpack; from it, he retrieved rope and a rappelling hook.

When at last—gasping and perspiring, despite the cold—Struker reached the bottom of the cliff, he turned away from it and trudged over the uneven terrain to the spot where he had seen his foe lying . . .

But the monk was not there.

THE MONK WAS NOT THERE.

Impossible, Struker thought; surely he had made a mistake. He had an excellent sense of orientation and had been very careful to note the body's position. Here, by the larger of two rocks, was the very place . . .

Yet he had to be mistaken. The monk no doubt lay elsewhere. And yet . . .

Struker could not resist the compulsion to walk as closely as possible to the spot where he had seen the monk fall.

Once there, he drew in a gasp. The signs were subtle, but unmistakable. There, on the earth, was a tiny spattering of fresh blood, and the imprint of his body, where he had lain. There, too, was the place he had set his hand, and pushed down in order to raise himself to his feet.

In fury and frustration, Struker lifted his bleeding face to the Himalayan sky and screamed. . . .

THE UNITED STATES

STATES

THE PRESENT

1

Waiting on the platform, Kar was already whistling a brisk, tone-deaf little melody by the time the subway car came screaming into the station. Bishop Square was his favorite station, and he watched as the doors of the train opened, and his plump and juicy prey came spilling out: Wall Street types, most of them, with thousand-dollar briefcases and glistening gold Rolexes on their wrists.

He hoisted his well-worn duffel bag over his shoulder and jostled his way into the crowd. He liked his work, he told himself; he was cheerful, he told himself. Today was just like any other day.

Truth was, for the past several weeks, a restlessness had come over him: he had begun to question himself, his life, why he lived as he did. This morning, he had crawled from his bed with an uncharacteristic tightness in his gut, a sense—was it foreboding, or anticipation?—that today every-thing was about to change.

He had scolded himself then: *Quit with the sensitive jerk stuff—so you feel your life is empty, blah, blah, blah. Quit letting your nerves get to you. You're just worried about getting caught, that's all. And it's not going to happen. You're too good.*

It was bogus, this sense of guilt—he hadn't exactly had an easy life. And he was at least decent enough to steal only from the rich—*me and Robin Hood*—who could easily afford to lose a twenty-thousand-dollar watch here, a Prada bag there, an Hermès scarf or a wallet loaded with cash and credit. *Hell, they're probably all insured.* At least they all had mothers and fathers—rich ones, most likely, who'd sent them to the best schools, given them every opportunity in life. And they had real names and knew their family history, and hadn't had to grow up fighting for survival on the streets.

Kar set to work. Not exactly the nine-to-five variety: this particular job required exquisite skill and even better timing. He conjured up a look of innocence in his wide eyes and "accidentally" bumped into his first victim: a guy in a three-piece gray pinstripe Armani and polished wing tips that cost more than Kar's annual rent. Kar brushed an elbow against him, slipped a hand into the guy's rear pocket—too quickly for the victim to feel, much less see—and deftly slipped the captured wallet into the duffel bag.

Victim number two: female in high-heeled

Manolo Blahnik pumps, wearing a diamond Rolex. Kar pumped up the charm, accidentally brushing against her arm, then smiled in apology—such a dazzling little grin that she smiled back, oblivious of the fact that her Rolex was now safely inside the duffel bag.

Kar turned away, slightly disgusted. He bore no ill will toward the young woman, but—diamonds, no less. The watch must have been worth thirty, forty grand . . . and people in the city were going hungry.

He turned to his next mark, scarcely noticing the person itself, only the pocket, bulging with cash, that called to him from a pair of nearby khaki pants. Almost of its own accord, his hand fished into the pocket, effortlessly withdrew a wad of cash . . .

. . . and was immediately slapped with a steel cuff. A snap, and suddenly both hands were cuffed.

Kar stared up into the face of his intended mark: a uniformed cop, who held the chain leading to the cuffs tightly in a large, thick-fingered fist.

"You picked the wrong pocket to pick, prick," the cop sneered. He was a large man, broad-faced, broad-shouldered, used to intimidating others with his bulk. Beside him, Kar looked like the skinny kid he was. Anyone standing on the subway platform with spare change to bet on the outcome of the encounter would have put all their money on the cop.

Kar was not in the least bit shaken: he'd made the same mistake before, with similar results. For an instant, he regarded the policeman with a purely pleasant expression.

And then he spun around, hands a blur, moving so quickly his eyes could not even follow what his own fingers were doing—but his brain knew, and that was all that mattered. He snatched the key from the burly man's grip and wriggled his hands from the cuffs, then just as swiftly slapped one on the cop's wrist and the other one to a railing.

Before the policeman could even register what had happened, Kar favored him with his best, boyish Kar grin. "Sorry about that, Officer. Nice cuffs." His tone wasn't particularly sarcastic; Kar in fact *was* sorry that the cop had caught him, and forced him into the unpleasantness. And they *were* nice handcuffs: cold, quality steel.

He took off into the crowd, listening with one ear as the officer pulled out a walkie-talkie and shouted into it. "Officer needs assistance! Perpetrator on foot, heading northbound on Bishop Square platform! Repeat: northbound on Bishop Square platform!"

Outside on the street level, the dirty sidewalk was filled with rush-hour commuters, all hurrying to make their way home; a few stopped at the corner newsstand to make a quick purchase of a magazine, a newspaper. One man among them, however, stood calmly studying a headline: from him radiated a sense of quintessential stillness. He was in no rush to go home; it had been destroyed by Germans some sixty years before, followed shortly by the Chinese Communists.

Yet in all that time, the monk had not aged: his hair was still jet black, his face unlined, his body as strong and firm as it had been the day his beloved master transferred the power of the scroll to him. Indeed, the overcoat he wore, acquired soon after he had made his escape to the West, showed more signs of his travels than he did himself: the fabric was shiny, almost threadbare in places.

And, slung over his shoulder, he still bore the bamboo case that housed the sacred scroll, just as he had every day for the past six decades.

He read the headline silently to himself, after many years finally accustomed enough to the English language not to have to translate the words into Tibetan first: UNIDENTIFIED ASIAN MAN PULLS THREE FROM FIRE.

He felt no sense of achievement, of self-congratulation at having done a good deed. The people would have died otherwise; it was the responsibility of all those on the path to prevent suffering wherever possible. He was only fulfilling his karma. Perhaps, in one of his previous incarnations, he had been trapped in a burning building, and one of those souls had rushed in to save *him*. Perhaps he was doing no more than returning a favor.

In one sense, however, the headline disturbed him. It reminded him that he felt unfulfilled; it was his duty to find and train a successor, and thus far he had found no suitable candidate.

And five times the Year of the Ram had come and gone.

The monk drew in a slow, even breath and dismissed the thought. Such concerns were a form of grasping. When the time was right, the student would appear.

In the interim, the monk lifted his gaze slightly above the newspaper's edge, with its incriminating headline, and looked beyond, to the sidewalk on the opposite side of the street. There, a hardened-looking man wearing a dark suit and barely detectable earpiece smoked a cigarette. To most, he no doubt seemed perfectly calm; but the monk saw clearly his nervousness. He had encountered this cigarette-smoking man before, and knew him to be a mercenary; as the monk continued to surreptitiously watch, two more dark-suited mercenaries joined the first man. They spoke quietly together . . . and the monk knew himself to be the subject of conversation.

Silently repeating the Vajra Guru mantra, the monk drew in another calming breath, then gently manipulated his neck in order to stretch it. When he glanced back at the newspaper headline—then took stock of his surroundings—he realized that two more men in dark suits now stood only a few feet away from him in front of the newsstand. Casually, they began leafing through *Soldier of Fortune* magazines.

The first three mercenaries started across the street, for the stand.

The monk took note of the glances exchanged between the five men.

He had always wondered why his master had insisted on martial-arts training; he had never understood, until he had come to this wild country, why a monk would ever need training in anything other than meditation.

The five dark-clad mercenaries closed in on him, hunters closing in on prey.

With a violent sweeping motion, the monk scattered his newspaper at them, causing paper to fly in their faces, cover their eyes and mouths, buy an instant of distraction.

It worked. The men clawed at the paper, tore at it, cast it down and aside. Once freed, they encircled the monk, surged forward at him, fists raised.

One man swung; the monk ducked, then launched himself into their midst, flipping from feet to hands to feet again.

The one who seemed to be the leader swung again at the monk; again, the monk dodged the blow skillfully—with the result that the leader wound up hitting one of his own men.

A well-placed kick, and another mercenary went flying into the newsstand, bringing down a cascade of paper that half buried him.

The monk spun and ran.

Instinct led him down into the bowels of the city, into the subway station.

Behind him, the voice of the leader rang out. "Get him!"

The monk increased his speed, hurrying down to the station. It would have been wiser to lose himself in the city; there were few places to hide in the subway, especially if no trains happened to be arriving or departing at an auspicious time. Yet he felt drawn, with a certainty he had learned long ago to trust, to head southbound at Bishop Square.

Behind him, his pursuers' steps rang out on the stairs.

At the same time, Kar was still heading north— this time at full sprint, gasping beneath the weight of his overstuffed duffel bag. It had been a good day's haul, and he wasn't about to let himself get caught with it.

He also couldn't afford to slow; the cops were still in pursuit—at least two of them at last backward glance. And they seemed to be gaining on him.

For the first time in a long time, Kar let himself feel afraid. Maybe this was what the unsettled feeling he'd had for weeks was trying to tell him: that he was going to get caught, and that he might as well give up his life of crime now, for good.

That hardly seemed an option at the moment. Jail seemed a more likely outcome. He couldn't exactly stop in midstride, turn to the nearest cop, hand over his duffel bag, and say, *"Here, Officer, just take this and let's call it even, shall we?"*

And go off to start life afresh.

Not going to happen. And then, in the midst of his mad, anaerobic dash, Kar felt his fear transform into something very different, very odd: a sense of destiny, as if for the first time, he was no longer running *away* from something, but running *toward*.

On the other end of the same platform, the monk was likewise running at top speed from his pursuers . . . but very quickly saw his way blocked by a crowd waiting at a broken turnstile. A repairman crouched over it, tinkering away with a small tool.

The monk could not let his progress be hindered. He reached into his pocket for a token, then launched himself upward and vaulted over the broken turnstile, flipping the token to the repairman as he flew past.

As he ran off, a glance over his shoulder confirmed that the dark-clad mercenaries were not so polite: they had brazenly drawn automatic weapons and were now brutally shoving their way through the terrified crowd.

In the midst of his high-speed dash, the monk felt pity for the innocents being pushed and frightened, all because of his presence here; even more, he felt pity for the mercenaries pursuing him. They had been paid to do so, and—caught up in the hypnotic pull of this world, of samsara, with its illusory glittering riches—they did not know the truth of who and what they were pursuing, or why. He longed to cease his running, to stop and explain these things to them, that they might have better understanding . . .

. . . but he had tried to do so before, at other times, with other pursuers, with near-disastrous results. He did not fear death: he knew, as his master had taught him, that death could bring the greatest bliss, so long as the soul was prepared. But he dared not die without finding his Next, and he knew the mercenaries would not stop to listen to explanations. They would fire their weapons.

He could elude most bullets—in fact, he had eluded all of them since 1943, when he carelessly permitted one, fired by the Nazi commander, to strike him.

Most of all, he dared not stop because he saw before him, on the crowded platform, many more innocent souls awaiting the next train; and he hoped fervently to bring them no harm.

And then the monk registered an odd sight: someone running *toward* him from the opposite direction. Not a mercenary, for he could sense such things about human beings; his training permitted him to see beyond the façades people wished to present, into their souls, and see the goodness or evil there.

A man—perhaps twenty years old, pale-skinned,

with cropped brown hair—both deeply good and deeply troubled, was fleeing with his own burden slung over his shoulder: a worn duffel bag. Despite his speed, he wormed his way through the crowd with considerable physical skill, a grace that reminded the monk of the martial-arts exercises he had performed with his brothers.

Farther beyond came his pursuers: the police, a sight that surprised the monk. So this young man was a criminal . . . ? How could he have so misjudged him?

Yet another sight worried the monk. He realized, with an abruptness that permitted him to take no action, that both groups—the mercenaries chasing him, and the police chasing the young man—were about to meet. And he noted, with concern, a young mother, oblivious of how perilously close she and her six-year-old daughter stood to the platform's edge. The mother, smiling and unaware of the two groups bearing down on her, knelt down to adjust her daughter's shoe. The child stared down at the affected shoe, her gaze innocent and somber, a doll clutched in her hand.

In the space of less than a human heartbeat, the collision occurred: one wave of human flesh struck another, with a group of commuters caught in between. The young man and the monk both managed to spin themselves free of entanglements of arms and legs and bodies, but policemen and mercenaries both plowed into professionals, with disastrous results.

As the crowd swelled to the edge of the platform, the little girl teetered on the precipice above the tracks. The monk watched with horror as, rather than let go of the doll and use her arms to fight for balance, she grasped the doll harder, fearful of losing her treasure . . .

Grasping, the Buddha said, is the root of all suffering.

. . . and plunged downward, onto the train tracks.

"Katie!" the mother shrieked, with such ferocity it could be heard above the din. The crowd quieted at once; mindful of the police, the mercenaries holstered their weapons at once and lost themselves in the crowd.

Even before they left, the monk had already leaped down onto the tracks.

Oddly, he was not surprised to find that the young man with the duffel bag leaped down at precisely the same instant. Both men hurried to the little girl, her face red and tear-streaked, her arms still wrapped about her doll.

During the fall, her tiny ankle had become twisted and wedged firmly beneath a steel railroad tie.

The tunnel filled with the wind and roar of an oncoming train.

The duffel bag still slung over his shoulder, the young man stared down, lips parted, brow furrowed, in despair. His expression indicated clearly that he saw the girl's situation as hopeless . . . and nonetheless, could not bring himself to leave her lying in the path of the train.

The monk knew better: he had been trained to see hope in the most hopeless of all situations, possibility in the midst of the greatest impossibility. Over the roar of the coming train, he shouted at the young man.

"Grab her leg—get ready to pull!"

The young man hesitated. On his expressive, handsome face the monk saw played out the battle between grasping and surrender: the duffel bag contained items very dear to the young man, items he was reluctant to part with.

But the struggle was brief, and the goodness the monk had detected in the young man won. He tossed the duffle bag aside, and with both hands took hold of the girl's leg, firmly but tenderly.

On the platform, an awestruck crowd watched in silence as the distraught mother screamed again. "Oh my God—*help her! Help my baby!!!*"

With detachment, the monk noted the increased rushing of wind and noise, the growing vibration beneath his feet as the train neared. He drew in a deep, calming breath, focused his mind on the Buddha, and ran his fingers over the railroad tie.

At last, he wrapped his hands around the tie and began to pull.

The young American watched in stunned disbelief as the railroad tie trembled—not from the approaching subway car, but from the monk's impossible effort. The monk ignored all—the sound of the train, the young man's gaping stare, the crying child—and remembered only the Buddha. Only the Truth. He pulled harder, but felt no effort.

The thick steel yielded slightly upward, just enough so that the young man slipped the girl's leg free with ease.

A policeman on the platform watched the entire event in amazement; had he not been surrounded by a crowd, which included two of his fellow officers, he would have doubted what he had seen. He knew well enough that eyewitness accounts were often faulty and suspect, including his own.

But too many people saw what he saw: the perpetrator—of all things, a perp who'd had the nerve to slap an officer in his own cuffs!—and an Asian man jump onto the tracks to rescue the little girl. The Asian had to have been some sort of martial-arts wizard—bending the tracks with his bare hands, leaving the perp to pull the little kid free.

It had been a miracle, and the frantic mother had cried aloud in joy . . . then, all too cruelly, the train had roared into the station, bearing down on them. There'd been no time.

The cop considered himself tough; he felt he'd seen it all. But at that moment, he'd closed his eyes, and wished he'd been able to close his ears, as well, so that he couldn't hear the mother's agonized screams.

The train—the express, no stops—had howled by.

There followed a second of aghast silence, in which the cop opened his eyes, but couldn't bring himself to look down. Beside him, someone tried to grab the mother and keep her face averted, but she wrenched free.

The policeman steeled himself and looked down at last; it was his duty to take control of the situation, to call for paramedics to remove the bodies, to protect the crowd and move it away from the tragedy before anyone else fell onto the tracks. One of his fellow officers had already made her way to the scene and was trying to comfort the hysterical mother.

But the bodies he expected to see weren't there. No mangled perp, no Asian man. . . .

And on the opposite platform, tousled but unharmed, stood the little girl, alone and squalling at the top of her lungs.

Her doll, the only victim, lay crushed on the tracks between them.

2

In the darkness of the empty subway tunnel, the footsteps of the monk and the young American echoed, mixing with the rumble of a distant train.

"Sonuvabitch!" the young man swore. He seemed honestly angry at himself. "I lost my whole stash!"

Apparently he referred to the duffel bag and its contents. "Be happy," the monk told him. "You helped save a human life." He judged the American's anger over lost material possessions to be superficial. He remained convinced that, deep down, the young man was filled with a goodness that could never truly regret helping another.

But the American's tone remained huffy; he turned a boyish, handsome face toward the monk. "Yeah, well, last time I checked there's no reward for that." He fell silent a time, then, with a different tone—this one of grudging respect—asked, "Tell me somethin' . . . how'd you do that back there?"

The monk considered asking which particular action he referred to—the bending of the steel, or the preternatural speed with which he hurled the three of them out of the path of the train, and up onto the opposite platform—then decided it did not matter, as his answer to either question would be the same. He shrugged. "Practice."

The young man let go a gasp of sarcasm mixed with disbelief, then stopped moving abruptly. "Who the hell are you, anyway?"

The monk faced him squarely. "That's not the question you need to ask. You should be asking who *you* are."

The American blinked in confusion. "Excuse me?"

"Your mind is filled with compassion," the monk explained. "That's why you risked your life to help that child. But your mind is also impure— so you forget the spiritual reward and think only of the financial."

The young man's lips twisted in disbelief. "Oh, yeah? If you're so 'pure,' why were all those guys in suits chasing *you*?"

The monk felt his body tense slightly; fear rippled through his normally calm mind, like a pebble cast into a still pond—not for himself, but for the American. This was not a question he could answer without endangering the youth. "It doesn't concern you."

The American persisted, shoving his face into the monk's, taunting. "Let me guess: FBI? CIA? DEA? ATF? INS? IRS?"

The monk had heard only of the first two organizations, and the last—the middle three he could only guess at; but the young man's doggedness troubled him. It would not be wise for this young one to learn too much. . . . In a stern tone, he repeated, *"I said it doesn't concern you."*

He turned and headed away swiftly—too swiftly for the younger man to follow—into the shadows.

And there came a step—an instant when one foot met the hard man-made ground of the station—that the monk's heart rid himself of fear, and saw the truth.

His master had taught him long ago that coincidence was mere illusion; and his meeting with this young stranger, so good-hearted yet so confused, had been no coincidence. This young one had helped him save a life, and here the monk was reacting unkindly toward him, out of the basest of instincts: fear.

And with that step, the monk pivoted, his expression softening, and walked back to the young American.

The youth turned back toward him, gaze vaguely suspicious.

"I'm . . . sorry," the monk told him softly. "Every man's life concerns every other man—especially if he's on the Noble Path to True Enlightenment." He paused. He was not used to speaking about himself, but at this moment, it seemed the proper thing to do. "I'm very tired . . . a little desperate . . . and running out of time. I'm afraid I took it out on you. Will you accept my apology?"

The American's eyes—so young and yet so jaded, so innocent yet so full of guile—widened in unfeigned surprise. His thoughts flitted visibly across his expression: *This guy is* apologizing? *For* what? *Is he serious?*

Then he composed himself—or at least, made an effort to keep a straight face—and said thoughtfully, "That's some deep shit, man. All right . . ." He offered his hand. "Apology accepted."

The monk moved to take his hand . . . and was startled when the American wrapped his arms around him instead and hugged him tightly.

The impetuosity seemed inappropriate, but the monk, out of a desire to be courteous, returned the embrace—in his country, more appropriate for long-lost relatives than for strangers one had just met.

The hug, too, seemed overlong. But at last, the American drew back, tears shining in his eyes. He spoke, his voice thick with emotion. "Sorry, man. Sometimes I can get a little . . . emotional—you know?"

The monk studied him calmly and saw no emotion, only guile. The embrace had been as contrived as the tears in the young man's eyes; but for what purpose?

"No problem," the monk replied, still regarding him curiously.

The youth did not linger; he gave a swift, cheerful wave, then strode off down the subway tunnel, clearly anxious to be on his way. The monk paused, watching—then, shaking his head in amusement, turned and walked off in the opposite direction.

Kar moved quickly to put as much space as he could between himself and the kung-fu character as quickly as possible, before the Asian dude had the chance to realize he'd been hustled. Kar figured the guy owed it to him: he'd been forced to lose all the booty in his duffel bag, after all . . . so much for good deeds paying off. But at least the day hadn't been a total waste . . . maybe, if the piece of Hong Kong paraphernalia he'd just lifted was worth anything.

Kar began his tuneless little whistle, and tried to let the effects of the adrenaline fade from his body and mind. He'd been trying to focus on his anger over losing his stash in order not to admit the obvious: One, that he'd been terrified as hell that his goody-two-shoes nature had very nearly cost him his life a few minutes ago; and two, that he felt he and the monk had somehow met before, which was purely ridiculous. Okay, make it three: Not only did he feel he somehow knew the monk, he felt that the monk was the cause of the anticipation he'd been feeling for the past few weeks. That somehow—somehow, the monk understood him better than he, Kar, understood himself, and knew the purpose that was missing from his life.

Bullshit, of course. All bullshit.

Kar shook his head mentally at his train of thought—then was suddenly distracted from it altogether when two dark, forbidding figures stepped toward him from the shadows.

He made a move to turn—too late. One of the goons grabbed him, and before he could spin free, the other one landed a right cross to his jaw that sent him sailing backward into a darkness even more profound. . . .

In the meantime, the monk was still headed in the opposite direction, but beginning to experience a sense of unease, which indicated he had somehow veered outside the proper flow of karma.

Perhaps he had been too quick to leave the young man; perhaps he was destined to help him in some way. There was something compelling about him, something which convinced the monk that they had met in a previous incarnation.

The monk stopped in midstride, considering this—and then froze altogether as another thought struck him. He reached for his bamboo case, flicked it open . . . and felt the blood drain from his face.

The scroll was missing.

Her name was Jade, and she spent her life by day pretending she was something she was not: hard-bitten, uncaring, with a heart that could no longer be broken.

Her father had broken it often enough. And so

she had decided years ago, as a little girl, that she would become tougher than her father, harder, colder; no man would ever be able to break her, but she would be able to break any man she chose.

She hung with the dregs—people her father, had he still been living at home, would have said were beneath her. He preferred her in her Ivy League background; he had wanted her to become everything that he was not . . . but she determined to become the one thing he was—a criminal—because that was the only way she could break *his* heart.

At the moment, she was hanging with Fuktastic and his crew. Obnoxious name, Fuktastic, and scarcely the Ivy League intellectual her father had always wanted to see her with. Still, he was shrewd enough: a sinewy, broken-nosed Cockney who'd grown up fighting on London's streets, and had a keen mind where capitalism was concerned. His outrageous success was matched only by his arrogance: across his hard-muscled chest, he'd branded himself with an oversize tattoo: MISTA FUKTASTIC. He had the hots for her, but for the time being was willing to be led on with mere whispers and promises.

Perhaps it was because he knew, the way every other member of Fuktastic's gang knew, that she could whip any of their asses any time she chose. In that way, she was an outsider: privy to all of the crew's secrets, and to Tastic's favor, yet she paid no dues, owed no loyalty, followed no orders, and came and went as she pleased. Because Tastic liked her—and perhaps even feared her a little—the crew paid her the utmost respect.

The night everything changed for Jade, they were hanging in Fuktastic's headquarters—the old subway warehouse, filled with rusting caterpillar tractors, old railway ties, and empty trains, not to mention the dirt, rats, and spiderwebs. Physically, she was exhausted, though she kept that to herself: she'd been training harder than usual lately, challenging herself to master the most intricate martial-arts moves, meditating longer than usual, chanting for a full hour.

She'd been close to giving up meditation before that night; insights had begun to flood her mind, insights she didn't particularly like, in the form of questions.

Why are you consorting with these criminals? Are you truly able to pay back your father by doing so? Or are you merely hurting yourself?

That morning, during meditation, an odd thought had popped into her brain.

Tonight is the time. Be open to the change.

At the moment, she had managed to push any thoughts of meditation aside, along with any silly notions of mystical changes, and was settled atop some rusty equipment in the subway warehouse, along with the rest of Tastic's crew: Pee Wee, a weasely little street-gang dropout; Sax, the second-in-command, who fancied himself an intellectual and student of Machiavelli; DV, a coffee-skinned androgynously turned-out chick, a total techno-brain; Buzz, a witless hulk, the org's muscle; and Diesel, a chip-toothed psychotic with a frightening penchant for sharp blades and a definite need for medication.

All of them were staring upward, at their Glorious Leader, Fuktastic, who stood atop a large forklift, one arm wrapped around an unhappy victim's neck—another gang leader with the currently unlikely moniker of Tough Guy; Tastic's other arm terminated in a formidable fist, which was pounding the hell out of Tough Guy's midsection.

Fuktastic's shout echoed through the vast warehouse. "How many times do I have to tell you people? NOBODY"—he punctuated each word with a blow—"ROBS . . . ANYBODY . . . IN . . . MY . . . TERRITORY . . . EXCEPT . . . *ME!*"

As he spoke, DV, her dark brow furrowed in concentration, squinted down at her palm-sized LED code-breaker in front of an ATM—one that Tough Guy's gang had ever so kindly managed to rip from the wall of the local bank. Jade glanced at her in admiration; you could almost see the sparks crackling around DV's head as her brilliant brain fired, synapse after synapse. If she ever decided to use her amazing mind for good—

Jade interrupted herself in disgust. *What kind of pansy-ass thought is that?*

Up on the forklift, Tough Guy had broken free and, bloodied but defiant, shouted back. "What the hell are you talk' about, Fuktastic? That ATM wasn't in your territory!"

Tastic favored him with a crooked grin. "I'm happy to report my territory is *expanding*." Gracelessly, swiftly, he planted a kick so powerful in Tough Guy's gut that Jade could hear the muffled sound of ribs cracking; Tough Guy went flying backward off the forklift, slammed down against the ground, hard, and went out cold.

Simultaneously, DV grinned as the teller machine in front of her lit up like a slot machine and started spitting out bundles of cash. She glanced up proudly at Tastic. "Jackpot."

The other crew members exchanged low-fives with her, then she immediately started counting up the cash.

Still on the forklift, Tastic signaled to the lean and dark-eyed Sax, who threw a switch. With a grating whine, the lift slowly descended.

As it did, Pee Wee whipped out his ever-present can of spray paint and tagged the sprawling Tough Guy across the chest with Fuktastic's symbol, insulting the unconscious gang leader as he did so. "*Rallado!*"

Fuktastic climbed off the lowered lift and stepped forward as Sax yelled to the crew, "Next!"

Court was in session.

Sax tossed his boss a washcloth; regal as any monarch, Fuktastic delicately wiped the blood and sweat from his fingers while a couple of his crew dragged the unfortunate Tough Guy outside.

Jade shifted where she sat. Her muscles ached from her earlier workout; she was tired, she told herself, and bored, not in the mood for the meaningless, testosterone-laced antics of King Fuktastic's court tonight. She wanted desperately to go home.

Out of habit—damn meditation!—she stilled her mind, and was forced to confront the truth of her thoughts and feelings. Yes, her muscles ached, but she was neither tired nor bored. She was nervous, because she was filled with an odd anticipation she did not understand.

And so she sat.

And watched as Shade—tall and lean, a pair of knobkerries, Zulu war clubs, strapped to his back—dragged in the next victim, and dumped him on the floor in front of Fuktastic.

Just another young tough, nothing special. White, spiked brown hair, sort of Irish-looking. Cute, if his face weren't bruised and bloody.

Yet at the sight of him, Jade touched the amulet around her neck, made of the precious stone for which she was named. She leaned forward, moved as if to call his name—then realized she did not know it, even though she felt she should.

Sax cleared his throat, then frowned at the long list he had penned on the inside of his olive-skinned forearm. Like a bailiff in a courtroom, he read out clearly: "Finger-man. Calls himself Kar . . ."

Shade provided additional information. "Caught him ripping off marks at the Bishop Square subway station."

Fuktastic finished cleaning off his hands, then with a flourish tossed the dirty washcloth to Sax. Jade watched keenly as Tastic turned his full attention on Kar, then gave his fresh victim a pleasant nod.

"I've heard a lot about you, Kar—how nice that we can finally meet. Fuktastic's the name, profit's the game. Now I know you're *new* in town, so maybe you haven't heard how I operate. You see, I'm a businessman. And my fiscal policy toward crime consists of two words: *zero tolerance . . ."*

Car, Jade thought. *What kind of guy names himself after an automobile?* Despite his grim situation, Kar scanned the room with a confidence that seemed oddly genuine—sizing things up, Jade realized, checking out the competition. Trying to see what he could get away with, who he could take down.

And then he met Jade's eyes. She tried her best to look away in time, to affect boredom—all in vain. Kar caught her gaze and locked in on it; there was the faintest spark in his eye as he realized he intrigued her . . . and there was no doubt in her mind that the attraction was mutual.

At last, she forced herself to look away, to feign interest in what Fuktastic was saying.

". . . unless of course," Tastic was lecturing Kar, "the criminal in question has an officially authorized Mister Fuktastic *franchise."*

Kar grimaced. "Franchise? You sayin' I'm supposed to *pay you* for the right to rip people off?"

Sax, ever the details man, chimed in. "Sixty percent, off the top." He ignored Kar's outraged gasp and continued. "This entitles you to squatter's rights at Mister Fuktastic's cribs, chow at his greasy spoons, and protection provided by Mister Fuktastic and his crew."

Buzz, who had hurried to Shade's side the minute he brought in the prisoner—in hopes there might be trouble—leaned menacingly over Kar. "That's *us*."

To his credit, Kar didn't flinch, didn't squirm, didn't move a millimeter from his position. Instead, he flashed a dazzling smile at Jade—who struggled hard not to be undone. What *was* it about this guy that made her feel an instant kinship with him? She wasn't the type to fall easily for anyone . . . in fact, she'd never permitted herself to fall for anyone at all. She did her best not to return the smile.

With admirable ease, Kar surveyed his surroundings, then answered lightly, "Sorry, but if this is a good example of a 'Fuktastic crib'—I'll be checking into the Motel 6."

Despite herself, Jade grinned; Kar caught it and grinned wider.

Fuktastic laughed, too—a hard, cold sound that had nothing to do with humor. "Oh, that's good, Kar. That's *really* good. . . ."

He struck the young thief hard in the gut; with a groan, Kar dropped to his knees and held his midsection.

Fuktastic's tone turned quiet, deadly. "You'd be a corpse already—if not for the fact I hear you're an exceptionally good earner. But maybe I heard wrong—maybe you *can't* help me earn my *bees*. In which case . . . you're nothing to me. Less than nothing. And around here, 'less than nothing' . . . means *dead*."

Kar lifted one arm beseechingly. "Okay, okay, man—chill out! You heard right about me. Here . . ." He dug beneath his shirt, and withdrew a faded piece of rolled-up paper. A scroll, Jade realized . . . and then, when Kar unrolled it slightly, she caught sight of what was inscribed there.

Tibetan calligraphy—unmistakably authentic, and apparently very ancient. No doubt it had come from a monastery before the Chinese had invaded Tibet. Jade leaned forward, electrified; from where she sat, she could not read what was written there, but she suspected the information was very important indeed. And Kar clearly had no clue as to its true value, or he certainly wouldn't be offering it up so easily.

". . . take this," he finished. "An offer of good faith."

Fuktastic, of course, had even less of a clue. He grabbed the scroll from Kar's hand and looked it up and down, his bottom lip curling. At last, he said, "What do you think I am, a bloody *tourist?*" He hurled the scroll across the room, and shouted, "Try to pass that made-in-a-Bangkok-sweatshop-piece-of-shit off on *me?!*"

"Man, that's the real thing," Kar insisted. "Ancient calligraphy! And about us doing business . . . how's . . . *forty* percent?"

The crew began to shake their heads at Kar's clearly fatal mistake; Fuktastic, too, shook his head and smiled in disbelief. "Gotta admit, you got big *orchestras*, Kar." The smile turned to a snarl. "Too bad I'm gonna have to cut them off."

Kar blinked at him. "I have no idea what you just said."

Diesel stepped forward, hand already on one of the blades sheathed at his hip, and gave Kar a wicked, jagged-toothed grin. "Your *balls*—he's gonna *cut off* your balls!"

Kar paled.

The distraction created by Kar's audience with the gang leader permitted the monk to slip into the warehouse unnoticed.

At last he knew the name of the young man who had helped him save a life—and now had stolen from him the only possession he cared to protect. Indeed, the monk had shuddered to see the scroll profaned as the gang leader so callously tossed it aside . . .

. . . but that had produced the very opportunity that would allow him to recapture it.

His gaze remained focused on the very spot where the scroll lay, and as the drama unfolded around him, the monk slowly, surreptitiously, began to move toward the sacred object.

In the meantime, Mista Fuktastic's henchmen were moving to surround Kar, who raised his hands in protest.

"Taz, man, that is *not* a good plan!" His tone had grown a half-octave higher with desperation. "You say you're a businessman, let's negotiate!"

Fuktastic shrugged. "I gave you your chance and you blew it. The only thing left to negotiate are the exact terms of your *funeral.*"

Jade squirmed where she sat. She did not want to see this Kar harmed . . . and yet she could think of no way to help him without being disloyal to Tastic.

Kar found her gaze again and held it; he tried, again, to summon up another one of those charming smiles, despite his agitation. "Excuse me, uh . . ."

She pretended to watch coldly; she did not help him out by offering her name. And so he made one up.

"Bad Girl," he said. "This seem like a fair fight to you?"

She smiled coldly at him. "Sorry, Kar. Life's not fair."

He gave a little shrug, quirked up one corner of his mouth. "Can't you see I'm just tryin' to make a living?"

She spoke out, perhaps more hotly than she would have to anyone else, simply because she was angry at herself for being so charmed by him, for being so sentimental as to believe they some-how knew each other, even though they had never met.

"All I *see*," she said, very distinctly, "is a cute punk who thinks he's hotter shit than he is and whose wise ass I can't wait to *kick*."

His eyes widened at that . . . and so did his grin. For an instant, he seemed to melt, like a lovesick puppy. "Wow. You think I'm cute and wise—plus you can't take your eyes off my ass."

She rose, eyes flaring, and turned to Fuktastic; she knew he would not deny her. "He's mine."

She did the simplest, most basic move, pulling up on Kar's arm and kicking his legs out from under him: it was all she needed to do, because she was fast, and because he wasn't expecting it.

He landed flat on his back. She dropped and straddled him, and swung back her arm, ready to deliver a blow to his head that would knock him unconscious (she was hoping that this would sat-isfy Fuktastic, and spare Kar)—

And stopped, in mid-move.

Kar just lay there, limply, not even struggling. Instead, he gazed up at her with a goofy, adoring grin.

If he didn't struggle, that would make her look bad in front of the crew. Furious, she whispered down at him, "What the hell are you looking at me like that for—don't you realize I'm about to beat the living shit out of you?"

He stared up at her, entranced; she could hear

the sound of his breathing. "Sorry. It's just . . . you're so damn beautiful."

That totally undid her. Not because of his words—words were cheap, and most people never said what they really thought anyway—but because he really *meant* them. They took her completely off guard . . .

. . . and in that instant, Kar—no slouch himself when it came to fighting, obviously—flipped her in a heartbeat, then straddled *her*.

". . . especially when you're *angry*," he finished, smiling down at her.

If she hadn't been so attracted to him, she could easily have killed him.

The next second, he was sprawling in the dirt, kicked there by a furious Fuktastic.

"*Wanker*," Fuktastic spat. He turned to his crew. "Kick his *Khyber!*"

The rest of the crew shoved past Jade and converged on Kar; kicking, shoving, punching, they hurled him up onto the second level of the scrapyard.

Kar was clearly no stranger to the martial arts; he spun and whirled, dodging most of the blows aimed at him—but he froze in place when he saw Fuktastic charging at him with an iron construction rod.

Once again, Kar found Jade's eyes.

She moved swiftly, quietly, so that the others, especially Fuktastic, would not notice her betrayal, and kicked another, shorter iron rod toward Kar.

He grabbed it just in time to deflect Fuktastic's blow; the *clang* was deafening.

"Give it up, Kar," Fuktastic sneered. "My pole's bigger than yours!"

He swung at Kar again. The heavy iron rods collided, throwing sparks into the air.

Again, he swung; again Kar answered the blow. Again. And again . . .

The noise of the furious duel afforded the monk his opportunity: ducking low so that he would not be seen, he retrieved the scroll, reverently replaced it in the bamboo case, and turned to flee—

Then stopped abruptly at the sight of several mechanical cranes, once used to salvage parts from the scrapped train cars, parked in a circle on the level above the ongoing battle.

A line from his master's prophecy returned to him.

"He will defeat an army of enemies while a flock of cranes circles above . . ." the monk whispered to himself. He paused to consider this, then shook his head. "Impossible. Besides . . . he's going to *lose.*"

Behind him, Kar let out a piercing, defiant howl.

The monk turned, and saw the young thief swing his iron rod in a wide, sweeping arc. Fuktastic and his crew could come no closer.

A fire began to burn in Kar's eyes; it was as though a different spirit had seized control of him.

Fiercely, fearlessly, he swung again and again with the heavy rod, forcing his enemies farther and farther back . . .

Until, at last, he forced them back into a corner. Then—with one triumphant, ear-shattering *clang*—he brought down his iron rod with such power that Fuktastic's rod split in two.

Kar howled with glee. The spirit of the warrior left him, and the spirit of the cocky young thief returned. In an effort to show his martial-arts prowess, he performed a rather amusing display with the rod . . .

And, his concentration thus broken, the rod itself slipped from his grip and went flying, leaving him disarmed and deflated.

He spoke in the small voice of a child. "Uh-oh."

Fuktastic smiled evilly as he lifted the broken pieces of his tire iron and prepared to smash them down against Kar's skull.

3

In an instant, the one Kar had called Bad Girl had wrapped herself around Fuktastic's shoulders.

Jade found the action less than appealing: while Fuktastic could be considered sexy, in a bad-boy sort of way, she had little respect for him—and thus she was far from turned on by having to come on to him. But it was the only way she could save Kar's life, short of killing Fuktastic and his crew herself.

So she did what she had to do.

"I'm bored with beatin' on this loser," she told Tastic in her sexiest voice. "Besides . . ." She slipped a tongue into his ear. ". . . fighting always gets me hot." She nodded her chin at Kar. "Let him go and let's party."

Fuktastic hesitated—then kissed Jade hard and full on the lips.

She fought to hide all signs of her disgust, and instead playfully snaked out of his grasp. She had no intention of having sex with him, of course—but he'd been so willing to be strung along in the past, he'd no doubt be willing to do the same again tonight.

Just as she expected, Fuktastic's arrogance got the better of him. He turned to Kar.

"Lucky for *you* this little piece o' crumpet's beggin' for some Fuktastic love. So while she's running the Union Jack up me flagpole, I want you to do some thinkin', mate—listen closely and don't lose the plot: me or my people ever see you boosting in my territory again, I'll snip your *hampton* clean off, shove it on a stick and serve it as a shishkabob." His tone turned deadly. "So get out. *Now.*"

Kar turned to leave—but not before catching Jade's gaze again. It was all she could do to remain beside Fuktastic, and not go with him.

From his hiding place outside, the monk watched as Kar slowly walked away from Mista Fuktastic and the red-haired girl. Memories from sixty years before had begun to flood the monk's mind, and he again whispered to himself a phrase of his master's:

"The most undisciplined youth I have ever laid eyes on . . ."

As the young thief walked from the warehouse, his back to the crew, the snaggletoothed one called

Diesel pulled a large blade from the sheath at his hip and hurled it at Kar.

The knife went whizzing past him—surely he was protected by the buddhas—and landed cleanly in the middle of an eye, painted on the crumbling wall.

The monk followed Kar outside, up out of the subway station and onto the city street. The commuters had long ago made their way home, and except for the passing headlights of the occasional taxi, the sidewalks were dark and free of pedestrians.

Kar soon turned down a side street, this one entirely deserted and bathed in the blinking glow from a dump truck's lights; the monk watched thoughts play over the young man's quickly shifting expression like clouds over a reflective lake. A slight grin crossed Kar's face at a memory; he whistled a bright, slightly off-key tune as he pulled a fist from his pocket . . . then opened it to reveal a necklace, upon which hung an amulet of jade.

The monk searched his memory: the young woman's neck, of course—Kar must have taken it during his struggle with her. She had been wearing the jade necklace before that moment, but the monk did not remember seeing it on her afterward.

He stopped in the shadows and began, softly, and then more loudly and rapidly, to applaud.

With a thief's instinct, Kar pocketed the necklace and spun around.

The monk smiled on him. "Congratulations on your victory," he said, without intending any sarcasm. "Though technically you were saved by a girl, it *was* your charm that convinced the girl to lead them away."

Kar scowled; in his eyes flashed a sudden anger. "Hey, mister do-gooder—if you were watching the whole thing back there, how come you didn't help me out?"

There was more than one answer to his question; the monk gave him the simpler of the two, the one he would most likely understand. "Because you stole from me."

"Oh, *that*." His anger left him at once, as if the monk's answer made perfect sense. His admission was so matter-of-fact, the monk's smile grew wider.

"But your fighting is very impressive. Where do you study?"

Kar shrugged. "The Golden Palace."

The monk drew back in amazement—he had not known this place existed outside of China. "You study with the Venerable Fighting Monks of Jin-Gong?"

It was Kar's turn to be dumbfounded; he stared at the monk in disbelief for an instant, then shook his head and started walking back down the street.

"Look," Kar said over his shoulder, "nice to share some more quality time and all that, but I gotta run. Sorry about stealing your . . . whatever-the-hell-that-thing-is. Good luck with that 'enlightenment' stuff."

The monk watched the young man as he walked past the strobing lights of a construction barricade.

Back at Fuktastic's, a rave was in session.

Jade, of course, refused all drugs, including alcohol—they interfered with the clarity of mind required by her martial-arts training and her meditation; besides, the last thing she wanted to do was to be around any of Tastic's gang without all her faculties intact.

The music was pounding so loud she could feel it reverberate in her teeth, and the crew was doing their regular thing. Buzz was down on the floor, bench-pressing Pee Wee (she wasn't sure who loved it more); Diesel and Shade were enjoying a little knife-versus-war-club choreography, a mock combat in time to the music. And DV—poor, lovelorn DV—was hip-hopping around Sax, hoping against hope that some day she'd distract him from his dog-eared copy of Machiavelli's *The Prince*.

As for Jade herself, she was wedged into a corner making out with Fuktastic. It wasn't that bad, really—for a guy who was supposedly tough, he was a good, sensitive kisser. And despite his rough looks, he kept himself clean. But things were growing a little too hot and heavy. Jade tensed, preparing to make yet another excuse as to why she had to suddenly leave . . .

. . . when Fuktastic slipped his hands down below her waist and squeezed tight.

"Not so fast." She pushed him away—a little too quickly at first, then tried to cover up by giving him a sexy little smile.

Fuktastic's patience had apparently worn thin. He grabbed her wrist—not at all tenderly—and pulled her close.

" 'Not so fast'? I've been tryin' to go the *ole hog* with you for a *bloody* long and hard time—but whenever we get close, you up and run out on me. Nobody knows where you go, what you do. Nobody knows anything about you."

She grew a bit nervous, but kept up the sexy smile, kept her voice low and seductive. "You know I'm worth waiting for." She slipped free of his grasp and walked away.

But Fuktastic followed, no longer willing to be put off easily. He reached out and grabbed her shoulder, roughly. His voice took on that deadly serious tone that always meant trouble. "I'm *tired* of waiting."

He forced himself on her, his body pressing hard against hers, his lips pushing hard enough against hers to bruise. For a moment, she yielded . . . long enough to maneuver him into standing on top of his hydraulic forklift. A kiss—that's all it cost her—and she snaked out a hand, hit the control button, and sent the lift up into the air.

Fuktastic went with it, of course—stunned at first, then fuming.

"Sorry, baby," Jade said sweetly. "You're on my list—but you're not at the top."

She headed off quickly, without waiting to hear his reply, and left him with his amused-but-too-afraid-to-show-it crew.

She was barely out of the warehouse when a sensation—or rather, a lack of sensation—made her stop and touch her throat.

"Shit."

For some odd reason, Kar had always felt more at ease in Chinatown than any other part of the city, as if he belonged there—northern European mutt though he obviously was. And as he hurried toward the once-grand but now decrepit Golden Palace Theatre, its name still glowing brilliantly on the marquee, he felt that pleasant sense of coming home at the end of a long, hard day.

But his thoughts were mostly focused on Bad Girl: he had not been faking it when he had smiled up at her, pinned beneath her, and called her beautiful. She was, in fact, the most beautiful creature he could ever remember seeing, with her sculpted feminine muscles, her flowing long red hair, her green eyes and elfin features. . . .

He'd been smitten at once, and even if he hadn't been able to flip her over, even if she had wound up kicking his ass the way she'd intended, he would have continued to smile, happy despite the pain.

But he was even happier now: she had felt the attraction, too. She had helped him out, twice, and he would do everything in his power to make sure he somehow repaid her.

Kar dashed inside the theater and headed quickly up the aisle, bathed in the flickering blue light coming off the big screen, where two kung-fu fighters were going at it, shouting at each other in Mandarin above the English subtitles.

Abruptly, the reel ended; the screen went white. And stayed white, because Kar was responsible for changing the reels.

The sparse audience—mostly Chinese—began to boo. A half-empty box of popcorn went flying past Kar's ear.

He made a smoothing gesture with his hands, as if to massage away their complaints. "Relax, folks, enjoy the intermission! We've got plenty of warm soda, stale popcorn and dried seaweed snacks at the concession stand!"

In reply, two soda cans fired toward him in rapid succession; he dodged both and raced to the lobby.

Once inside, he very nearly ran down Mr. Kojima, his frail Japanese landlord, who was busy sweeping candy wrappers off the worn carpet.

Kojima propped himself against his broom and scowled. "You're late, Kar—you missed the reel change! Anyone wants their money back, I'm adding it to your rent!" Not, *My God, Kar, what happened to your face? Have you been in an acci-*

dent? Did someone hit you? He was far too used to Kar showing up looking like he'd been in a rumble.

Kar waved his hands in a gesture of innocence. "I'm on it, I'm on it . . ." He stepped behind the concession stand and popped open a small cookie tin inscribed with Chinese ideographs, then pulled out several scraps of paper covered with Kojima's neat, careful lettering.

"And another thing," Kojima rumbled. "I'm through taking your messages! What do I look like, an answering machine? My name is Kojima—not *Sony, Sanyo,* or *Toshiba!*"

Kar shot Kojima a surly look, then turned and headed up the narrow, rickety staircase to the projection booth, muttering to himself, "Who ever heard of a Japanese guy owning a Chinese movie theater, anyway?"

Kojima might have been ancient, but he wasn't deaf. "I heard that, smart-ass!" he yelled up the stairs. "Who ever heard of a white boy *working* in a Chinese movie theater?! You got an answer for that? Way I figure it, Kar, you got two choices: You can sit on your butt and do nothing—or you can fly like a phoenix from the ashes of your pathetic life!"

Kar yelled back over his shoulder. "I'm flyin', I'm flyin'!"

He wheeled into the projection booth and flicked on the second projector, starting the next reel, then changed reels on the first projector, threading up the next film on tonight's bill.

Finished, he turned and sighed deeply, then headed from the booth into the storage area next to it: a place Kojima referred to euphemistically as "Kar's apartment." It was no more than some dirty walls and a floor, a bed, a chair or two, and a convulsive refrigerator, but it was home, all that Kar really needed. As he entered, the walls shook spasmodically from the rumble of a subway train passing below, but Kar hardly noticed.

With a sense of relief, he stripped off his sweaty, grimy shirt, tossed it in a corner, then emptied his pockets into the empty film can that served as a catchall for spare change. One item in particular made him proud: the green necklace he'd stolen from beautiful Bad Girl. At least the day hadn't been a total washout. . . . The necklace would guarantee that he would see her again. But at the moment, he was aching from the blows Fuktastic the Fukhead had landed in his gut, and the one his goons had planted on his cheek. Once the pain subsided a bit, he'd be free to think of *her.*

He headed to the fridge, got some ice cubes, and winced as he applied them to the bruises on his face.

And whirled as a figure stepped from the shadows on the far side of the room.

Kar dropped the ice cubes at once—they clattered onto the floor and skittered beneath the refrigerator—and prepared to defend himself, worried that Fuktastic had changed his mind.

It was the monk, the bamboo case still slung

over his shoulder, as if it were a permanent part of his anatomy. He was smiling, and eating a bowl of cereal. Kar's cereal, in Kar's bowl. Amiably, he said, "So *this* is the Golden Palace where you learned how to fight."

Kar's heart was still pounding from the adrenaline. He had liked the monk when he first met him, had felt strangely drawn to him—had even been sorry to see him go. But Kar definitely did *not* like anyone tracking him to his apartment, much less breaking in. *"What the hell are you doing here?"*

The monk continued to smile. Smile and munch on cereal. Between bites, he said, "I should have known the Venerable Monks of the *real* Golden Palace would never allow such sloppy technique."

Kar began to feel righteously pissed. He had no idea what the monk was talking about, but he didn't like the sound of it. "Listen, man, this is *my* place. Get out. Now."

The monk listened to Kar's words. Considered them for a time. And didn't budge.

"An enlightened man would offer a humble traveler shelter for the night . . ." He smiled through a mouthful of cereal. ". . . and share a quiet conversation over a bowl of Cocoa Puffs."

"Really?" An edge crept into Kar's tone; he took a threatening step forward. "Well, I guess I ain't that enlightened 'cause I was thinking more of kicking your freaky ass back to wherever the hell it comes from."

Once again, the monk weighed Kar's words. And

then he shrugged, and commented pleasantly, "For someone who says he wants to 'kick my ass . . .' you do a lot of talking."

Kar glared at the monk for a hard moment . . . then laughed aloud.

And in the next instant, he launched himself at the monk in an all-out kung-fu attack. He sliced a killer blow at the monk's throat. . . .

The Asian man stepped back easily, gracefully, and took another spoonful of cereal.

Kar let go a short, sharp screech and aimed a couldn't-miss kick at the intruder's head.

The monk crouched, ever so gently, not spilling a drop of milk.

Another blow, another kick, a two-legged all-out kick that sent Kar sailing directly at him. . . .

In each instance, the monk calmly stepped aside, watching the martial-arts display with detached interest and eating his cereal with singular relish. Kar aimed at least a dozen blows directly at him—and each the monk deflected or eluded, without ever spilling a single drop.

Exhausted, Kar collapsed into a chair and watched, stunned, as the monk finished off his cereal, scraping the sides of the bowl with the spoon—*clang, clang, clang*—to get every last bit.

There was nothing to do but concede defeat. "Okay," a sweating, gasping Kar told him. "Fine. Guess I can't *make* you get out."

Still damnably cheerful, the monk crossed to the refrigerator, took out a bottle of Tsingtao beer, and tossed it to a startled Kar, who still managed to snag it.

"Is that why those guys were chasing you," Kar asked wearily, " 'cause you crashed at their place and wouldn't leave?" It was a joke, not a very funny one, but he was curious about his mysterious intruder. The man seemed interested in doing only good—yet he'd somehow managed to get someone *very* angry at him. Angry enough to send a horde of assassins armed to the teeth with some very serious-looking guns; those guys had made Fuktastic's crew look like a bunch of amateurs.

"Something like that," the monk said blandly, in a way that told Kar it was nothing like that at all.

The refrigerator began whining and coughing again, clearly in its final throes; the monk turned to it, and laid his hands on it as if he were about to pray for its healing.

Damned if the humming and rattling didn't almost instantly stop. This was getting more interesting by the minute.

Kar stared at him, intrigued. "How'd you do that?"

The monk gave him another of his annoyingly inscrutable-Buddha smiles. "I used to work as a refrigerator repairman." He sat in the chair across from Kar. "I overheard people calling you—'car?' "

Kar got that a lot. "Spelled with a 'K,' " he explained. "It's Cantonese."

The monk tilted his head, studying his features. "Funny—you don't look Cantonese."

"It means 'family.' Figured I never had one growing up, but from now on I'll never be without."

"I'm afraid you're mispronouncing your name, sir," the monk said softly. "It should sound more like 'Ga.'"

Kar shot him a sour look. "Look man, it's *my* name, I'll pronounce it however I want. What about you—what's your name?"

"I don't have one," the monk said, his tone perfectly serious. He gazed about, not even trying to hide the fact that he was checking out Kar's place—and his gaze fell on Bad Girl's necklace, lying in the empty film can. Kar rose and stepped in front of it to block the monk's view.

What the monk had said made absolutely no sense. "What do you mean?" Kar asked.

"You gave yourself a name," the monk said matter-of-factly. "I gave mine up." He paused to cease his inspection of the apartment, then focused all his attention on Kar. "You said you have no family. Have you always been an orphan?"

Kar involuntarily tensed at the question; it brought with it too many memories, memories that brought with them pain. Over the years, he'd transformed the pain to an angry attitude that the world owed him something because of his suffering. Why not steal from those who'd had all the advantages he never had? He'd never experience the sense of love and belonging they had—so why not take from them what he could?

Stiffly, he told the monk, "To quote you: That's none of your concern."

The monk shrugged in the face of Kar's reticence, then pulled from his pocket Bad Girl's green necklace. Kar did a double take, almost swore; the monk's hands were even more swift and surreptitious than Kar's, the nimble hands of a pickpocket—and then some. What was this guy, some sort of magician?

The green amulet dangled between them.

"So," the Asian man asked easily. "Why did you steal that girl's necklace?"

Kar swiped the necklace back, and felt an uncharacteristic surge of heat on his cheeks. Why did this guy make him feel defensive, as if he needed to explain himself? And yet, he tried to explain himself anyway. "I didn't steal it! I just . . . borrowed it." The minute he said it, he felt embarrassed; it sounded like the explanation a child would give.

The monk eyed him skeptically.

"Look," Kar persisted, still not understanding why he found it necessary to tell this man the truth. "I think she's into me but I gotta cement the deal. I'm gonna track her down, return her 'lost' necklace—thereby placing me instantly in her good graces. *Deeply* in her good graces." He smiled at the memory of her, remembering the moment of instant attraction. More than attraction: it had been the same sort of unmistakable *knowing* he'd felt when he'd first seen the monk.

He'd *known* that she was meant to be an important person in his life, had known that from that instant things would never be the same for him again.

Kar grinned over at the monk, and tried to look and sound as if she were just another girl, another conquest. "It's foolproof."

The monk, his handsome features bland and unreadable, replied in a tone pleasant and non-judgmental—and yet his words were far from either. "Except for one fool—which would be you. If she realizes what you did, your entire plan will backfire."

Kar's smile vanished; he didn't answer, because what the monk had said had already occurred to him, and he had no idea how to deal with *that* outcome.

The monk did not wait for a reply. Instead, he rose and went over to Kar's bed—and without the slightest hesitation, stretched his body out on it with a sigh, and relaxed so deeply, so utterly, that Kar was as impressed as he was annoyed. But even as the monk relaxed, he kept the bamboo case right beside him; clearly, he never let it from his presence. Some sort of religious thing, no doubt.

"Gimme a break," Kar complained, moving over to him and staring down in disgust. *"You're sleeping on my bed?!"*

The monk's muscles remained free of tension, as if there were no angry tenant standing over him, shouting. He replied, his voice fading slightly as he drifted toward sleep, his tone that of a guest perfectly entitled to such hospitality. "It's quite comfortable, thank you."

Kar was altogether at a loss; unable to maintain his anger, he yielded. "If you're gonna sleep on my bed, you can at least tell me what's up with those guys that were chasing *you*."

The monk's eyelids, which had been slowly closing, opened fully again; he regarded Kar for a long moment, then nodded. "All right. Let me put it in language you'll understand." He paused. "Why do hot dogs come in packages of ten, while hot-dog *buns* come in packages of just eight?"

Kar clicked his tongue in disgust. "What the hell? You can't answer my question with another question—especially one as stupid as that!"

The monk shrugged, shoulders sliding up and down on Kar's tousled bed. "When you attain a state of enlightenment that allows you to answer *my* question, I'll answer yours." He gave a soundless sigh, then added pleasantly, "Good night."

He caught hold of the scroll beside him and tucked it safely under his arms—then, in a ritual that Kar sensed had been repeated thousands of times before, took an ancient locket from his jacket, pressed it to his lips, replaced it, and shut his eyes.

Kar stared at his visitor in disbelief for a moment, then opened his mouth to say something . . .

. . . and closed it again as the monk began to snore gently.

A few hours later that same night, the monk awoke, fully rested. The level of deep rest he had trained his body to attain allowed it to be fully replenished and energized on only two or three hours' sleep—a useful habit that permitted him to accomplish more than he might otherwise.

As a subway car rumbled beneath, the walls of the tiny apartment trembled. The monk rose, noting at once that Kar was gone. But from the crack beneath the closed door, a light shone from the projection room.

The monk passed through into the other room, and stepped up next to the projector. A reel of film was running, and the monk followed the path of the beam of light through the booth's glass pane.

On the theater's large screen, a martial-arts classic was playing, one the monk had actually seen many years before, when he had sought to understand how Americans regarded such things. *Descendant of Wing Chun*, it was called, and as the monk watched the familiar characters on the screen, he realized that the young American, Kar, stood poised atop the theater balcony.

On the screen, an actor lashed out against his opponent with a kick.

On the balcony, Kar answered—evading the kick with a graceful, swift duck, and replying with a slashing blow of his arm that would have disabled a living opponent.

The monk smiled. Kar had not lied: he did indeed hone his fighting skills at the Golden Palace. And to the monk's amazement, the young American was as talented, as quick, as lithe as any of the brothers the monk had seen trained in Tibet, many years ago. His encounter with Kar was indeed no coincidence, and was a blessing from the buddhas for both of them.

Unaware that he had been watched, Kar finished his grueling workout, then headed back up the narrow, stale-smelling staircase that led up to the projection booth.

He had long ago stopped asking himself what had drawn him so strongly, so irrevocably to the martial arts, and to Asian films, and to the Cantonese name he had chosen for himself; he certainly did not believe, as many of the films about fighting monks might suggest, that he did so because he had been Asian and involved in such things in a previous incarnation.

He did not permit himself to think about such things; religion was out the question, as painful a subject as thinking about his past. It was all wishful thinking, like hoping that one day he would find a family, a place where he fit in.

As silly as hoping that the Bad Girl with the green necklace could ever become a part of that family. As silly as hoping that the monk . . .

He quashed the thought at once, and ran the back of his hand across his sweaty brow, then opened the door to the projection room, and turned off the projector.

He opened the door to his apartment quietly, not wanting to wake the sleeping monk. . . .

But as the door swung wide, he could see that the bed, now neatly made, was empty.

And the monk was gone.

4

Inside the lobby of the spanking new Human Rights Organization Museum, Jade stood amid a crowd of journalists and television reporters and honored guests as well as visiting nobodies like herself, and stared up at the monument in the center of the cathedral-ceilinged lobby: a towering marble statue of a dove, holding a bronze olive branch in its beak.

The instant she had entered the building, an odd sensation had overtaken Jade: a creepy, skin-crawling feeling that things were *wrong* here, that they were not what they seemed.

Over time—especially now that she was meditating regularly along with her martial-arts training—Jade was becoming more and more prone to such feelings. The odd thing was, her intuition was always right, just like the intuition that told her that the thief Kar—even though he was a thief— was somehow a good guy.

Just as it was telling her now that the Human Rights Organization—to which she had been strangely drawn, for no apparent reason—was somehow very, very bad.

It was irrational, of course. But Jade kept her senses open as she followed the crowd inside the building, and listened carefully to the striking blond woman in the tailored suit who led them.

Smiling a perfect PR smile, the blond woman spoke, her voice echoing slightly off the vast ceiling and walls, her tone a little too practiced, a little too slick. "As executive director of the Human Rights Organization, I'd like to welcome you all to the opening of this new exhibit . . ."

Some exhibit. Jade shuddered at a row of beautifully framed sepia-tone photographs, displaying unspeakably brutal contents: a mass grave filled with bones and skulls; a torture victim, his bloody face mangled beyond recognition; a firing squad releasing a hail of bullets on shrieking women and children.

The executive director continued her spiel, her tone—in light of the heartrending exhibit—just a little too . . . Jade scoured her brain for the precise word. *Vivacious*. How could anyone be vivacious in the face of such atrocities?

"More than half a century ago," the director said brightly, "out of the rubble that was Europe at the end of World War Two, men and women of good will decided to build an organization dedicated to the prevention of human-rights abuses all around the earth. And today I'm here to tell you—" She paused dramatically to gesture at the various exhibits. "We *failed*."

A slight murmur came from the crowd at her unexpected admission. Reporters stepped forward with cameras to photograph the photographs; journalists jotted down notes. Jade continued to wander from picture to picture, her heart growing heavier at the sight of each one. How could anyone see such suffering and not want to end it?

And how could anyone bear the pain of knowing that so much suffering existed in the world? The very thought made Jade despair. . . .

"But we're continuing the fight," the executive director continued cheerfully, "the fight against hate, violence, oppression, and cruelty in all its forms. This new exhibit is a weapon in that fight— a fight we're hoping to enlist every one of you in."

She gave a nod, indicating that her little speech was over; then she stepped into the crowd and began to make small talk with a well-dressed couple, obviously wealthy donors.

Jade walked directly over to her and touched her shoulder. The mere act of contact with the woman's skin made her shudder, the same way she had when looking at the gruesome photographs. "Excuse me . . ."

The blond woman turned. Her makeup was perfect, expensive, her perfume overwhelming; the smile, frozen on her face, seemed suddenly harsh. "Yes?"

Jade gestured at the horrific imagery surrounding them. "Do you ever worry that some of the people who come here . . . will be inspired?"

"I hope and pray that every person who comes here will be inspired," the blond woman said brightly.

"No," Jade said. "I mean inspired . . . to do it *again*."

The executive director looked at Jade for a long moment. Her smile turned hard, and in her eyes Jade saw something that made her skin crawl. "Granted, there are a lot of sick people out there . . . but thankfully most of them don't attend our functions." She began to turn away.

Jade persisted. "I got an idea—how about instead of showing atrocities . . . you do an exhibit that shows man's *humanity* toward man?"

The blonde turned toward her again; an awkward moment of silence passed between them, and Jade sensed the dislike emanating from her. Truth was, Jade didn't care much for the blonde, either.

"You don't help anyone by protecting them from reality," the director said. She led Jade a few steps away from the couple, toward a larger-than-life photo of a uniformed Nazi execution squad and its instant-away-from-death blindfolded victims. "Look at this. . . ."

Jade looked in horror.

The blond woman leaned close in and whispered in Jade's ear.

"Deep down inside, at the bottom of your soul, who would you rather be? The one about to be shot . . . or the one about to do the shooting?"

A shiver ran down Jade's spine; she pulled away and stared in disbelief at the woman, whose lips were still curved upward in that cold, brittle smile. In her eyes shone a chilling light.

The moment was broken as the woman's beeper went off. She glanced down at it; from her reaction, the message was clearly *very* important.

"I've got to go," the woman said shortly, and without a trace of sincerity added, "I really enjoyed talking with you."

Jade watched, aghast, as the woman strode out of the building.

In the museum courtyard, the executive director of the Human Rights Organization watched as a black limousine pulled up directly in front of her.

The vehicle came to a halt; the doors opened. Inside sat a frail, aged man—a dying man, his profoundly wrinkled face obscured by an oxygen mask.

The director looked on him with a mixture of disgust and fondness; disgust for the putrefying blob of flesh he had become, fondness for all that he had taught her. As weak as he was now, he had taught her how to be strong—how not to flinch from what must be done, however distasteful. She had inherited his cold heart, and for that she was grateful to him.

She watched as his assistant, a muscular, dark-suited man, tried to lower him from the limo into a wheelchair; even then, the old man fought any help, angry at his own weakness. By an act of sheer will, he pushed his aide away, and, teetering perilously, managed to get out of the car and into the wheelchair by himself.

She looked on him with pride. This man, her grandfather, was used to strength. He had once climbed the Himalayas with no more than a rappelling hook and some rope. His will was so strong that she wondered at times whether he ever would succumb to death.

She moved over to him; he looked up at her and, from behind the mask, asked at once, "Have you found it, Nina?"

"Yes," Nina answered. She did not try to soften the truth; he would not have respected her otherwise. "Unfortunately, we also lost it."

He gritted his yellowed teeth and glared up at her with pure rage.

She did not quail; she did not react at all, except to take charge of his wheelchair and push him from the courtyard into the lobby of the Human Rights Building. During the ride, both remained silent; Nina let him chew on his anger for a time until, inside, he glanced about at the visitors milling about.

"I'm surrounded by weakness and failure," he said bitterly.

"No, Grandpa," Nina corrected him. "That was

before. Now I'm here—and you're surrounded by respect, admiration . . . and love."

She leaned down, gently pulled aside the oxygen mask, and kissed his withered cheek.

"We'll get the scroll," she said. "It's just a matter of time."

He glared up at her, gasping slightly, his features freed at last from the mask, and she could see the three scars left there some sixty years before. Claw marks, she knew: he had told her the entire story of his battle at the Tibetan monastery, of the amazing power he had witnessed there, and of his desperate search for the scroll.

"Time," Colonel Struker said, "is the one thing I'm running out of."

On a nearby crowded sidewalk, Kar was carrying two film cans in a bag slung over his shoulder, and two hot dogs in his hands—a little working lunch. He was trying to do his best to keep his mind on work, but it was difficult: thoughts of the beautiful, redheaded Bad Girl, and the mysterious monk, who'd disappeared without explanation, kept occupying his thoughts.

He rounded a corner, spotted a rich-looking young businessman in a three-piece Armani suit, and made sure to "accidentally" bump into him.

Kar juggled his hot dogs, pretending to be close to dropping them. "Shit!"

The Suit was annoyed. "Hey, watch where you're going!"

Kar scowled back at him. "Watch where *I'm* goin'? Man, you almost ruined my breakfast!"

The Suit shot Kar a dirty look, brushed some sauerkraut off the lapel of the Armani, and kept moving.

Once he was safely out of view, Kar smiled to himself as he whistled his trademark thief's tune and studied the brand-new designer wallet in his fingers. Nice, very nice. . . . He slipped it into his own pocket and took a huge, satisfied bite out of one of the dogs, then began to walk in the opposite direction.

This time, he bumped into a passing pedestrian *without* trying . . . and almost dropped his hot dogs for real.

It took him an instant to realize that *he* had just been the mark, for a pedestrian who had just taken the wallet Kar had stolen. He watched in disbelief as the pedestrian sprinted down the block and caught the Suit.

Damned if the pedestrian wasn't the monk. He bowed slightly as he handed the wallet back to its owner. "Excuse me, sir—I believe you dropped this?"

The Suit gaped down at it and began to thank the monk profusely. Again, the monk bowed slightly, waved good-bye, then walked back to Kar as if nothing extraordinary had just taken place.

Kar was furious. Stealing his bed was one thing—but stealing his loot, his livelihood, was another. *"What the hell was that?"* he demanded hotly.

The monk lifted a hand and shook his wrist. "Sleight of hand."

Kar had had enough. "I thought I was through with you, man. Now you show up again and you're pickin' my pocket?"

The monk remained cheerful and matter-of-fact in the face of Kar's anger. "The pocket was yours—but not what I picked."

They began to walk together, passing a homeless person panhandling. Kar flipped a few coins into the person's upturned hat, then turned his fury back on the monk. "Don't you have anything better to do than follow me around and screw up my attempts to make a little extra cash?"

The Asian man ignored the question, and instead studied the hot dogs with an expression of honest disgust.

"What?" Kar pressed. "You got something against hot dogs now? Last night you were using them to try and teach me 'ultimate enlightenment.' "

"I was translating universal truth into words you would understand." The monk gestured at the dogs. "But this—to keep the body pure one mustn't kill any living creature."

"I didn't kill it," Kar replied smartly. "I'm just eating it." And to annoy the monk further, he took a huge bite out of one of the dogs. "And by the way," he said, his words partially muffled by the food in his mouth, "I figured out the answer to your question from last night."

The monk did not attempt to hide his surprise, but gestured for Kar to continue speaking. Kar chewed a bit, swallowed, and then, quite impressed with himself, said:

"Check this out: The reason hot dogs come in packages of ten but hot-dog buns come in packages of just eight is so that you'll *always* need *more* buns for your hot dogs—because no matter how much you get, how much you achieve, how many times you win . . . you can never, ever let yourself feel like it's enough."

The monk stared blankly at Kar for a time, then said, "Excuse me."

And turned away.

For a while, Kar was forced to listen to the sound of the monk's riotous laughter. Oddly, there was no put-down in it, no sarcasm, just open good humor for the strangeness that was life, and for an instant, it felt so infectious that Kar thought of joining in.

Instead, he decided to be pissed.

After a moment, the monk, his black eyes shining, turned to Kar with a huge grin. "Not quiiiite right . . . but . . . good try."

Kar glowered at him.

The two continued walking through a courtyard area surrounded by a park, filled with workers having lunch, kids piling out of a school bus at the curb, and families with their kids, having fun.

Kar always noticed the families.

He forced his attention back to the monk. "For a

guy I barely know, you're really starting to annoy me."

The monk shrugged. "Knowing others means you're wise, but knowing yourself means you are enlightened."

Kar rolled his eyes. "Look, I'm enlightened enough already! *Enough* with all the fortune-cookie philosophy, okay? This is America—we don't have 'enlightenment' here, okay? We have Big Macs, strip clubs, shopping malls, Las Vegas and HBO—got it?"

And to punctuate his point, he stuffed the rest of the first hot dog into his mouth—which just barely closed around it—and chewed it triumphantly, defiantly, in the monk's face.

At that same instant, a strangely familiar, feminine voice called from across the street.

"Hey—you—Kar!"

He whirled about, and saw Bad Girl, her long copper hair gleaming in the sunlight, jogging over toward him from a museum building.

Kar panicked, chewing fast as a winter-starved squirrel to try to empty his overstuffed mouth; he wrapped up the second hot dog and slipped it into the cargo pocket of his pants.

With a small, discreet motion, the monk pointed to the corner of Kar's mouth.

Kar wiped the back of his hand across his lips; it came away mustard-covered, and he did his best to surreptitiously clean his hand off on his pants—just in time, as Bad Girl came bounding up next to him.

"Hey . . ." he greeted her, doing his best to sound casual despite the fact that her very presence made him melt. Had it not been for the hair, he might have thought he was looking at another person; her face was still incredibly beautiful, her body still sculpted to perfection . . . but the sultry, slightly angry attitude she'd had the night before was gone, as was the tough-girl makeup. Now she had a fresh-scrubbed, college coed look—which suited her awesome, milky skin—and instead of the sex-kitten low-cut leather lace-up vest and tight pants, she wore jeans and a simple top.

And she was still a total knockout.

"You don't look like the 'Bad Girl' you did last night."

She completely ignored his comment. "My necklace."

Kar shot a nervous look at the monk, expecting him to blow things by blurting out the truth—he'd returned that dude's wallet, after all—but fortunately, the Asian man remained silent.

"Uh—excuse me?"

Bad Girl narrowed her green eyes at him. It was clear she was suspicious, didn't trust him worth a damn. "Last night I lost my necklace. Something tells me you might have some idea how I could get it back."

Kar felt the monk's steady gaze on him, and did his best to ignore it. "I guess I could keep my eyes and ears open, see what turns up," he told Bad Girl. "But what's in it for me?"

He expected her to flirt with him, to come on to him—maybe give him a little of the attention she'd been showering on Fuktastic the night before. Instead, she fixed him with a hard look. "It belonged to my mom. Means a lot to me. I guess . . . I'd owe you one." Then she looked at the monk with an interest Kar envied. "Who's your friend?"

Jade had been glad to see Kar, of course—for more reasons than simply getting her necklace back. She was attracted to him . . . but it was far more than a physical attraction. Just as she'd felt the night before, the feeling that Kar was destined to become intricately intertwined with her life overtook her at the sight of him.

And it was more than just the sight of Kar this time that gave her an odd sense of déjà vu. The sight of the Asian man—from his coloration, build, his cheekbones and features, no doubt Tibetan—sent a chill down Jade's spine, this time a chill that recognized the presence of True Good, as opposed to the True Evil she'd sensed emanating from the director of the Human Rights Organization.

She *knew* this man somehow, just as she knew Kar.

"He's my personal bodyguard." Kar stepped back and pushed the monk in front of him, with that barely perceptible smirk that told her he was totally bullshitting her again. "Watches my back. He's an incredibly deadly Shaolin monk. *Ten Fingers, Ten Toes—Twenty Reasons to Die.*"

The Tibetan smiled and nodded, clearly relishing Kar's ridiculous explanation. Jade almost laughed aloud at the two of them, but instead she forced herself to scowl and look the "bodyguard" up and down.

"Hold up," she countered. "Shaolin monks shave their heads every day. You're no Shaolin monk." She narrowed her eyes at the man's haircut—short, above the ears and collar, the jet black hair trimmed to a narrow widow's peak above the forehead. He was indeed a monk, a fact which intrigued her even more, but not Shaolin. "Tibetan Buddhist, maybe?"

The monk gave her a blessings-of-the-buddhas smile, then looked at Kar. "This young lady is nobody's fool."

Jade smiled, and said, in perfect Tibetan, *"Thank you."*

The monk turned his head swiftly to stare at her in amazement; his lips parted slightly.

Jade continued in Tibetan, gesturing at Kar with her chin. *"So why are you really hanging out with him?"*

She asked it as though it was of only casual interest to her—but in fact, her heart was pounding.

At her father's insistence, she had studied the Mandarin language at the university—China, her dad had always said, would be the next big frontier. He had no interest in his native Russia—*overrun with crooks*—but he felt Jade had the business savvy for dealing with the Chinese. And he'd always wanted her to take over the family business.

Over her dead body, Jade had told him.

But she loved the language studies anyway. And when she grew out of pleasing her father, she dropped the Mandarin and instead found a wizened professor who was willing to give her private lessons in his native language—Tibetan.

He was also a monk, actually a *rinpoche*—a master of sorts, who'd once run a monastery in Tibet before the Chinese had destroyed them all. And he'd scared the shit out of her by telling her that she was the reincarnation of a very high-ranking lama, which was why she was drawn to relearn her "native" language, to become so proficient in the martial arts. He told her she had a very great destiny. . . .

She hadn't wanted to hear any more. He understood; he limited their conversations thereafter to language lessons. But afterward she had sought out every single book written on the subject of Tibetan Buddhism, and she had found a different teacher—one who did not speak to her of her destiny—to teach her the Tibetan form of meditation.

Now, as she looked at the monk, the memory of all her teacher had said came back to Jade.

The monk smiled as he answered Jade's question about Kar. "*Somehow I sense he has a lot of potential.*"

"Really?" Jade laughed. "*I sense he's mostly full of shit.*"

This made the monk's grin widen. *"Maybe. But rich manure can fertilize fields which will feed millions."*

Perhaps the monk had a point; Jade considered his words.

As she did, Kar could keep silent no longer—apparently, being totally left out of the conversation had driven him crazy. Even though he had no clue what was being said, he suddenly chimed in, his tone knowing. "Yeah, *tell* me about it."

Both Jade and the monk turned to regard Kar curiously. Jade could no longer hide her true feelings—she giggled, honestly charmed by Kar's childlike desire to appear cool. As she studied him, she permitted a slight smile to play across her lips.

"You know," she said, her tone light, "last night was the first time I ever saw anybody stand up to Fuktastic. Incredibly brave and incredibly stupid at the same time. Interesting mix."

Kar stared back at her, obviously equally charmed and, for once, at a loss for words.

Kar was beyond smitten; Bad Girl's—or Not-So-Bad-Girl's—emerald gaze enveloped him completely for an instant, so that he saw nothing else, knew nothing else. It was trouble, he knew, to let himself fall so utterly for a girl, but this time he couldn't help it. Besides, this time, he'd fallen harder and differently. There was something— God, he sounded like a sappy chick—*pure* about this, something beyond pure lust. He'd never experienced a sensation quite like this before.

He scarcely noticed, scarcely heard as a huge city bus went roaring off right behind them. . . .

He only noticed, when the monk slapped his arm, bringing him back to reality, that a team of dark-suited mercenaries—the same mercs who'd been chasing the monk in the Bishop Square subway station—was crossing the street, headed directly for them.

"Go, *now!*" the monk ordered, and took off running.

Kar sized up the situation and instinctively grabbed the film cans from his bag and hurled them at the approaching mercs' feet like bowling balls. Some toppled over, like pins; but those still on their feet came right at Kar.

He shot a last, longing glance at Bad Girl. "Hey—I don't even know your name!"

She opened her mouth to answer, but before he could hear what came out, he was forced to break into a full run to stay ahead of his pursuers. He put it into overdrive, and somehow managed to catch up to the monk. But the mercs were perilously close behind . . .

. . . and, at the same time, more Dark Suits started racing toward them from the opposite direction. It was a total setup.

"Shit!" Kar swore, then turned to the monk. "Sorry, pal. This is your fight, not mine. Good luck."

He veered off down a side street . . . and kept running like hell. He didn't intend to slow down until he was safely out of sight, around the corner. . . .

But the instant he made it around the corner, he saw a fresh group of Dark Suits at the end of the alleyway, heading for him.

Kar ducked behind the nearest trash bin, cursing under his breath. Then he made a decision, straightened, and took off running back the way he'd come.

5

Running at top speed, Kar watched from an ever-shortening distance as the monk tore through an empty city street, only a few steps ahead of his dark-suited pursuers. Even though Kar still had no idea why these men were chasing the monk, he'd come to think of the Asian man as a friend—who else would eat his Cocoa Puffs without asking, and sleep in his bed?—and Kar knew instinctively that he could have done nothing wrong.

Whoever the dark-suited dudes were, they were bad news. And Kar would do whatever he could—which probably wasn't much—to protect his friend from them. At the very least, he could show support by letting himself be chased by the same bad guys.

What was it Bad Girl had said? Incredibly brave and incredibly stupid. Yep, that was about the size of it.

As he watched, the Suits started pulling out

their automatic weapons. Make that *beyond* incredibly stupid, with a death wish.

Kar emerged from behind a building to rejoin the monk—although the two of them were separated now by a chain-link fence.

Kar called to the monk—probably the last words he'd ever speak, and the monk would ever hear. "I thought about it, man. Couldn't just leave you hangin' like that."

In reply, the monk abruptly vaulted over the fence—practically sailing up into the air, à la *Crouching Tiger*—and landed on his feet at Kar's side. Dumbfounded, Kar somehow kept himself moving, and the two of them raced side by side toward the end of the block.

Good news . . . and bad. The street ended in a busy intersection, loaded with traffic that both provided witnesses and blocked them from escaping. Kar skidded to a stop.

But the monk, amazingly, never even slowed. He ran, timing his steps so that the oncoming traffic barely missed him—and then, as Kar gaped, he ran intentionally, directly, into the path of an approaching car . . .

. . . and up onto the hood, just as the driver swerved to avoid hitting him . . .

. . . and instead plowed directly into the dark-suited mercenaries.

The impact from the car sent the Suits flying backward; the pistols, shining silver in the sun, flew from their hands.

The monk snatched the weapons from midair, then vaulted off the car onto the street.

For a long moment, the monk stood facing the two mercenaries who had managed to struggle back onto their feet. The guns in his hands, the monk aimed them point-blank at his pursuers. Kar gaped, not daring to breathe. The Suits cowered in the face of certain death.

A shadow passed over the monk's features . . . then vanished, as the calm of enlightenment replaced it. Swiftly, the monk ejected both clips into the faces of the two Suits, knocking them both unconscious. They dropped like stones to the sidewalk.

But behind them, other Dark Suits were coming to take their place.

"This way!" Kar shouted.

He spun around and raced down another alley. The monk followed . . . and, unfortunately, so did the mercenaries.

Gasping, Kar shouted at his friend. "These are the same guys who were chasin' you in the subway, right? They don't give up easy!"

"They haven't for sixty years," the monk called back.

Kar's jaw dropped; he stared at the monk for as long as he could without tripping over his own feet. *Sixty* years? What the hell was the guy talking about? He couldn't have been more than thirty years old, tops. . . .

An odd thrill passed through Kar. He'd known,

the first time he'd seen the stranger, that there was something strange about him, strange in the sense of wonderful, mystical. Bad Girl had picked right up on the fact that he *was* a monk, just as Kar's instinct had told him. A Tibetan monk, guarding a mysterious scroll.

And it just so happened that his destiny somehow intersected with Kar's.

Maybe the monk *had* been running for sixty years. The question was, from *whom?*

The unlikely pair, American and Tibetan, continued running through the city streets, at last making their way into Chinatown—territory Kar was more familiar with.

He was just beginning to feel confident they had lost the mercs when, out of nowhere, a Dark Suit stepped out in front of them and aimed his automatic pistol at the monk.

He fired, and Kar felt his own heart freeze in his chest.

The bullet came whizzing directly at the monk—who sidestepped it neatly; Kar flinched as it struck the building beside them, sending a chunk of brick flying.

The Suit fired again. And again. And again.

The monk dodged each bullet in an intricate dance of gracefully moving arms, legs, and torso; at times, it seemed as though his body waved in the air like a chaff of wheat in the wind. And each time, Kar winced as the bullet struck nearby, sending bits of debris flying, at times missing the monk by the merest of millimeters.

With each bullet, the monk danced ever closer to the source of the bullets . . . until at last, he stepped up to the startled mercenary and knocked him unconscious with a single blow from the side of his hand.

Kar opened his mouth to congratulate the monk . . . but immediately closed it again at the realization that, farther down the street behind them, a fresh team of Dark Suits were racing toward them.

Damn! The monk was right. These guys *didn't* give up. . . .

The monk shot a glance at Kar and pointed to a nearby storefront window—from the wares displayed, some sort of pottery factory.

"Inside," the monk said, in a tone that allowed for no further discussion. "Now!"

Kar didn't argue. The two of them hurled themselves inside the door just as the mercenaries outside spotted them and opened fire.

Gasping as he lay with one cheek pressed to the cool floor, Kar gazed with open admiration at the monk. Jade was right—he *was* a monk, and not just any old Buddhist brother, but some sort of special master with powers that were damned near magical. Kar had seen some pretty impressive martial artists in his day, but *this* guy was beyond any of them.

"Man," he told the monk, who turned his face to look at his partner. "You're *good*."

The monk flashed him an incandescent, more-charming-than-Kar-could-ever-hope-to-be smile, revealing even, white teeth. "Why, thank you."

In the next second, he sprang to his feet, pulling Kar up with him, and hustled him past the pottery displays and a curtain, into a back room.

At a round table, a group of elderly Asian ladies sat playing dice. One silver-haired, heavyset woman lifted an arm in the air and rattled the dice loudly in a cup, then slammed it down on the table with an even louder exclamation—not in Chinese, Kar decided; he had some familiarity with the language. No, this had to be Tibetan, the language the monk and Bad Girl had been speaking not so long ago.

At the sudden arrival of Kar and the monk, the old ladies turned to stare at them owlishly. The monk gave them all a polite nod, and again smiled that disarmingly bright smile.

"I'm looking for Brother Tenzin."

This was apparently the right thing to say: the ladies all broke into approving grins, as if the monk was their long-lost nephew.

A mere sixty seconds later, the dark-suited mercenaries all came piling into the back room of the pottery factory, guns exposed, and glared at the old women.

No sign of the monk, or the kid who'd been with him.

But one of the mercs called out as he spotted the back door, swinging open in the breeze.

All of them were captivated by the sight of the open door—so captivated that none of them noticed that one of the worn wooden floorboards under their feet protruded ever so slightly. . . .

With a final glare at the women, Struker's men went racing out the back door.

Beneath them, peering up through the pinhole cracks between the floorboards, Kar felt his heart hammer as the mercs paused. . . .

Then, as they finally all went trampling away, he breathed a deep sigh of relief.

He looked down, and turned. Beside him, the monk was smiling at a handsome young Asian monk, this one dressed the part in crimson and saffron robes.

"Brother Tenzin," the monk said, with reverence and affection.

Brother Tenzin graciously bowed his head. "Brother With No Name."

So it was true, Kar marveled; the monk really didn't have a name. And it was clear from the way Brother Tenzin bowed and spoke that the monk was especially respected.

Kar followed as Brother Tenzin led him and the monk deeper into the basement.

At the end of a dark corridor stood a secret temple, lit by hundreds of candles and butterlamps. Kar did his best not to look totally amazed, but it was difficult; in the temple, some twenty Tibetan monks were either silently meditating or performing a series of exercises that looked vaguely like yoga.

At the appearance of the monk with no name, a murmur passed through the group; the monks who were moving ceased, and those who were seated in silent meditation rose. All turned to regard their nameless brother with deep awe; then, one by one, with a rustling of saffron robes, each monk bent forward in a low, reverent bow.

Kar was growing more impressed by the moment with his new friend—but he still managed to catch the look that passed between Brother Tenzin and the monk. Tenzin looked skeptical; he shot the monk a look that clearly said, *Who is this outsider?*

The monk nodded, his expression was one of utter reassurance—but even then, Brother Tenzin lifted a skeptical black brow, then gestured toward a door hidden farther back in the shadows of the temple.

"Allow me to offer you a place to freshen up," Brother Tenzin said, "and a jar of our finest Lhasa yogurt." It was clear his invitation did not extend to Kar; monks with no name only, please.

The monk motioned for Kar to stay put, and followed Tenzin through the doorway.

Kar did his best not to be insulted—but he was

a little ticked off anyway. If he was good enough company for Brother With No Name, who obviously ranked high on this monastery's list, then why didn't Tenzin trust him?

He was only slightly mollified when one of the other monks—this one no more than a skinny kid, Kar's age or younger—approached him and bowed low in greeting.

"What's up?" Kar said pleasantly. He moved toward him and instinctively tried to engage him in a little hip-hop dap, with a few high-fives mixed with low-fives, some bumped elbows and a hammered fist or two . . . but the kid-monk just looked at him as if he were insane.

Definitely not streetwise, this one. Kar shrugged and stuck out his hand to shake, in the old-fashioned howya-doin'-guy manner.

The young monk immediately took Kar's hand, and said, "Sky. Sun. Moon." He grinned suddenly as he pointed up at the basement ceiling with his free hand. "Street."

Kar gritted his teeth and tried hard not to squirm. Little Buddha's grip was like a *vise*, unbelievably strong.

But Kar had no intention of letting go.

And then the young monk's grip went *beyond* viselike; Kar winced with pain, and this time he *did* squirm. But he still refused to release his grip on the Asian kid's hand; in fact, Kar increased his own grip, and gave the young monk a look of pure challenge.

Yeah, keep it up. Let's just keep squeezing until one of us cries uncle—or Buddha. . . .

Inside a prayer room adjacent to the secret temple, the monk sat quite comfortably in the lotus position on the floor. After many years in the West, he still did not understand the Western craving for soft furniture—for overstuffed chairs and couches and soft beds, all of which kept the body weak and led to misalignments of the spine. It was far more comfortable, and strengthening to the spine, to sit on the good, firm floor and use one's own muscles for support. No wonder Americans were always complaining that their backs hurt—and no wonder so many of them had weak, sagging bellies.

It was good to sit on sacred ground again. He was very grateful that young Brother Sogyal—white-haired now, but he could only think of Sogyal as young—had come to this country with him, and founded this wonderful monastery.

Across from him sat Brother Tenzin—like the monk, enjoying a jar of yogurt. Above them hung a Tibetan prayer flag, inscribed with a passage from one of the monk's favorite scriptures, the Heart Sutra, which spoke of the inherent emptiness of form:

. . . in emptiness, there is no form, no feeling, no perception, no consciousness: no eye, no ear, no nose, no tongue, no body, no mind . . .

no ignorance, no end of ignorance up to no old
age and death, no end of old age and death, no
suffering, no origin of suffering, no cessation of
suffering . . .

The Heart Sutra always reminded him that, in the end, this world, samsara, was only illusion; all beings had already attained enlightenment, and all that remained was for them to see it. Eyes, ears, nose and tongue, body and mind . . . these things were all passing things, impermanent, and the day would come when he, too, had passed from the earth.

In the meantime, the monk listened politely to Brother Tenzin's question.

"Tell me, Brother . . . who is the boy?"

The monk answered the best way he knew how: with the truth. "He's a thief."

"A thief?" Brother Tenzin set down his yogurt and drew back. "And you bring him here?"

"Water which is too pure has no fish," the monk replied.

But Brother Tenzin's dark eyes remained troubled. "Yes, I see. . . . It's just—my master told me about that day in the Temple of Sublime Truth, sixty years ago, when you protected him. He was just a child . . . but he never forgot what he saw that day—the wonders of the scroll."

The monk set down his own yogurt. The memory still remained the most powerful of his entire life; he could still recall how the very air itself began to sparkle with the pure light, the pure power, of illumination. He could still feel its electric vibration surging through his body.

Tenzin continued. "All this time . . . we've been preparing. Now the Year of the Ram is upon us . . . and we have a number of very apt pupils right here at our humble temple—including one very strong candidate." He paused, his tone becoming slightly ingratiating. "I'm not saying it was *his* aura which led you here today, but then . . . you did get here, didn't you?"

The monk heard the grasping in Brother Tenzin's tone; clearly, Tenzin had in mind a particular young monk whom he wanted to become the Next. The monk understood; he might be guilty of the very same thing himself—except for the fact that he was perfectly willing for Tenzin's candidate to become the Next, if this was his rightful karma.

But it was the monk's duty to remind Tenzin of certain criteria that had to be fulfilled. "It's not a matter of study alone. There are the Prophecies."

A furrow appeared between Brother Tenzin's dark eyebrows. "But surely you agree, the Prophecies could not apply to the people of an unenlightened land such as this."

The monk regarded Tenzin solemnly for a long moment. "The Prophecies must apply to everyone . . . or they mean nothing."

Brother Tenzin returned the monk's gaze directly. It was clear that he did not like his elder's response—but he was also too honest to contradict the truth when he heard it.

He gave a slow nod. "Of course."

Inside the secret temple, Kar and the one he thought of as Kid Monk were still going at it. Maybe the Kid had had years of training at a Tibetan monastery—but it was still a dead heat. Kar was holding his own, not bad for someone who'd gotten all his training from Hong Kong movies and the city streets.

Even so, Kid Monk had taken him well beyond his usual pain threshold; Kar could only wonder how he was ever going to slip his poor, crushed hand inside someone else's pocket.

Just when he thought he could bear no more, he caught sight of the monk entering the temple. The monk moved toward the wrestling pair and motioned to Kar that it was time to get moving again.

Kar asked no questions—you would've thought the monk was his master or something—and immediately loosened his grip on Kid Monk's hand.

Kid Monk was at least a fair fighter; he immediately loosened his grip as well, then took a step back and bowed to Kar.

"Next time, brother."

Kar smiled and returned the bow. "Next time."

He moved to the monk's side. The nameless one was returning farewell bows to the other monks as he headed for the stairway leading back up to the little old ladies and their dice game.

But before he took his first step up, the monk paused to smile at Kar. "You helped me get away from those men. Maybe there's some help I can give you—with your fighting."

In the periphery of his vision, Kar saw Brother Tenzin and Kid Monk listening in—and from the looks on their faces, the monk's words did *not* make them happy. He couldn't imagine what that was all about . . . but he was thrilled at the monk's offer. He gave his soon-to-be master a huge grin . . .

. . . then grimaced in pain at his hand, which was red and throbbing. He shook it out. *"Damn!"*

The monk studied it an instant, then said, "Here." And he drew from his jacket a small jar of a thick yellow paste, and handed it to Kar. "Special medicine."

Kar gave it an uncertain look, then opened the jar and rubbed some on his pained hand.

He'd expected Tibetan Ben-Gay . . . sort of soothing and warming—but this stuff was far beyond that. To his amazement, it caused the pain to stop abruptly. He held up the hand and studied it as if it were a miracle. "Hmmm . . . Cool. Comfy. Fast-acting. This stuff is great!" A little funky-smelling, maybe, but awesome.

The monk smiled proudly. "Homemade—from my own urine."

Kar paled. He immediately scraped what paste hadn't been thoroughly rubbed into his skin back into the jar, closed it, and handed it back to the monk.

Nina walked into the control room of the Human Rights Organization and saw that Grandpa Struker, his oxygen mask in place, was slumped back in his wheelchair, his eyes shut.

The old man looked positively corpselike, and for an instant, her pulse quickened with hope. Perhaps he was dead . . . perhaps now she would no longer have to kowtow to him, to play the role of the adoring granddaughter in order to get what she wanted. . . .

She walked up to him slowly, aware of the clicking of her high heels on the floor. If he was in fact asleep, it wouldn't do to have him wake up to discover she was trying to see if he was dead. It had been hard enough earning the small amount of trust he placed in her.

She closed in, and glanced at the artifacts—more ancient than he was—and yellowed newspaper clippings that surrounded him, all giving accounts of a mysterious Asian man helping someone, then disappearing before he could be found. The obsession had fueled Struker all these years . . . an obsession his own son had refused to indulge, calling his old man sadistic, insane.

But his granddaughter had studied the clippings herself, and had begun to believe. If Struker was telling the truth—and clearly, there *was* a monk out there, performing amazing feats of rescue—then Nina wanted the power of the scroll.

She leaned silently over him and looked down at the scrapbook lying open on the desk in front of him. It contained photographs of experimental subjects—some with their eyelids removed, to see the effect it would have on their sleep patterns, some with great gaping sutures across their foreheads, where bits of brain had been taken . . . again, to see the effect.

All very scientific. And the scientists involved were Nazi Germans or Imperial Japanese. . . .

Behind her, Struker spoke; she gasped and clutched a hand to her heart.

"Did you know," Struker asked, in an uncharacteristically strong voice, "that during World War Two, Unit 731 of the Imperial Army conducted as many scientific experiments on their prisoners as Mengele did on his?"

Nina stared at her grandfather. Behind his clear mask, Struker was completely alert and wide-eyed. She began to suspect that he had never been asleep at all.

He continued his speech. "A brilliant team of these scientists was working to meld modern technology with ancient mysticism. Their goal was to lay bare the *'kami'*—the soul—of their enemies. Some say they were able to trace enemy movements and predict enemy action by stripping images, numbers, words from the minds of their prisoners—just before the prisoners died . . . horribly, of course."

"Of course," Nina said blankly. Her cell phone rang; she answered at once. "What is it?"

She listened to the reply . . . and a cruel smile spread slowly over her face. She turned off the phone and gazed, pleased, at her grandfather.

"We've got them," she said.

6

Jade made her way into the Golden Palace Theatre—hardly a palace anymore, or golden; the lobby's faded carpet had popcorn kernels ground into it, and it smelled like rancid butter. She made her way to the concession stand, watched a small cockroach crawl indifferently over a vacuum-sealed package of peanuts, then studied the elderly man watering down the syrup in the soda machine.

Oblivious of her presence, he was small-boned and slight, with delicate features that made her decide he was Japanese. It might have been a Chinese theater, but Jade had long ago begun to notice the marked difference between Asian groups: most people of Chinese descent were taller, larger-boned, with a less pronounced profile and more brown in their skin tone. The phrase *They all look alike to me* always made her want to come out swinging. Koreans, Thais, Vietnamese, Chinese, Japanese: all were distinct in their appearance and culture, and she resented the fact that most other Americans didn't care enough to take note of the differences. Had she mistaken the Tibetan monk for a Chinese, she would have been embarrassed; any unenlightened Tibetan would have been angered by it, since the People's Republic had razed their homeland.

"Excuse me . . ." she called politely to the old man.

He turned and glanced over at her—and saw a potential customer. "Yes, what can I get you?"

"I'm looking for someone—his name's Kar? I asked around. Heard he works here."

Annoyance crept over the Japanese man's features, even as he flattered her. "What's a pretty girl like you want to see him for?" Obviously, there was no love lost between Kar and his employer.

"Think he might be in trouble," Jade said, allowing her brow to furrow with the concern she honestly felt, and hoping the old man might soften.

But Kar's boss only soured further. "Damn right he's in trouble—half the day's gone by and he still hasn't got back with tonight's movie!"

Now Jade became even more worried; she leaned closer over the glass concession case, warm from the display lights shining down on the products. "You're saying he hasn't been in all day?"

The old man shook his head, and in a flash, Jade read him: Despite his attempts to play the curmudgeon, he, too, felt affection and concern for Kar. It was all an act, so Kar wouldn't think he was too soft and try to take advantage of him. Despite his anxiety, Kar's boss did his best to ease both his and Jade's concerns. "Don't worry," he told her reassuringly. "Kar can take care of himself—that's part of why I trust him to help me keep this place running."

Now Jade was curious; she smiled faintly at the old man. "What's the other part?"

The old man shrugged, apparently a bit uncomfortable with saying something good about his employee. His scowl softened ever so slightly. "I don't know why, but I can't help thinking . . . that kid's got potential."

Jade let her smile widen into a grin; she liked this crusty character. "So they tell me." She pulled a pen and a slip of paper from her jacket, jotted down some information, and handed it to Kar's boss. "Will you make sure he gets this?"

Back to the crotchety curmudgeon guise. He looked at the paper with a feigned sense of outrage. "What do I look like—a secretary?"

Jade turned on the charm. "Please."

He gave a grudging nod and took it from her.

She flashed him her best smile, then headed out of the lobby. As she did, the old man called sarcastically after her, "You're *welcome!*" And then he obviously read the slip of paper; she grinned to herself as he read aloud, " 'Bad Girl'?"

* * *

Kar stared up through one of the numerous skylights in the industrial warehouse the monk had brought him to. It was a sunny day, and the light warmed the room—a good place to work out, Kar reflected. Plenty of empty space, and the warmth was good for preventing pulled muscles.

Lord knows, he didn't want to pull any muscles, and have Brother With No Name whip out a jar of his homemade urine salve.

The monk stood in a pool of sunlight, speckled with shining dust. "I've trained Brother Tenzin's students here before."

And he began a series of martial-arts exercises, moving from sun to shadow and shadow to sun. "You must learn the unity of opposites," he said. "Be mobile *and* stationary—defensive *and* offensive."

Kar had read the same gobbledygook somewhere before, in his personal studies. It made as little sense to him now as it had then. But when the monk motioned for Kar to take his best shot, the young man tried to keep the thought in mind.

And he charged directly at his newfound master, arms slashing, whistling, through the air.

He made a little bit of contact—not much. The monk blocked every single blow.

And as he did, the Tibetan said, "You attack with all the wrong weapons, Kar. It's not about anger. It's about peace. It's not about power. It's about grace. It's not about knowing your enemy. It's all about knowing yourself."

And as Kar watched in amazement, the monk executed a series of totally gravity-defying leaps; it was as though he was flying through the air.

He landed, drew a deep breath, then smiled at Kar. "You try."

Kar did his best not to look aghast at the very thought. Instead, he molded his features into an expression of pure determination, then launched himself into the air . . .

. . . and fell flat on his ass.

The monk, blessedly, did not laugh. Very seriously, he said, "You fight too heavy. You need to fight *lighter*. The air—you can't see it, but it fills your lungs. It's as real as blood or flesh or bone or earth or water. Once you realize this, you treat the air the same way. You step on it as you would a stone, you swim through it as you would the sea." He flashed Kar a serene smile, as if he had not just been talking utter nonsense. "All you have to do . . . is *believe*."

Kar didn't even try to pretend that he bought what the monk was saying. "Believe what—that the laws of gravity don't exist?"

The monk remained implacable, infinitely confident. "If you truly believe that they don't . . . then they don't."

Now, *this* was some major Tibetan Buddhist hogwash. Kar shook his head, and opened his mouth to protest—

—but the monk raised a warning hand for silence, his eyes focused at a point beyond the frosted, floor-to-ceiling glass windows that lined the walls of the warehouse.

Kar followed his gaze.

The image was slightly distorted by the glass—but Kar still recognized the dark silhouette of a helicopter. What the *hell* was a helicopter doing so close to the building?

In the next instant, he got his answer.

The large windows erupted into a hail of shattered glass, accompanied by bullets, as the helicopter pelted them with machine-gun fire.

There was no time for thought, for decisions. Kar's body reacted before his dazed mind; caught in a crystalline blizzard that reflected the sun dazzlingly, he squeezed his eyes hard shut to protect them against the glass, then dove alongside the monk for cover behind some abandoned equipment.

In the next heartbeat, the monk seized him by the shoulder and pulled him—with such force that Kar's feet barely touched the ground—through a doorway, and down into the stairwell.

At that moment, they both froze. Two Dark Suits were running up the stairs toward them . . . and in the Suits' hands were some particularly large, deadly-looking automatic pistols.

This time, Kar moved on his own, in perfect synchrony with the monk. The two hurled themselves backward, back into the scarred loft, strewn with glass shining diamond-bright in the hard sun.

Behind them, the stairwell reverberated with a

deafening blast of gunfire; the wall that Kar had stood in front of a mere second before was gouged by bullets.

Kar's fear was devastating; he'd faced angry cops before, the occasional mark who pursued him angrily, but he'd always outrun them. But these Suits just kept coming—and they were well financed, judging by the quality of their clothing and weapons. And a *helicopter* . . .

This monk was facing some serious shit. Someone very evil, and very wealthy, was after *something* he had—something so incredible, they didn't care if they blew away the monk and Kar in broad daylight. Hell, they didn't even worry about blowing away the top of a building in the middle of the city.

In the middle of all that was happening, things began to make sense to Kar. No wonder the monastery was hidden . . . and no wonder Brother Tenzin had been nervous about outsiders being tipped off to its existence. But just what were these monks up to? What did they possess?

As Kar scrambled alongside the nameless monk to retrieve his coat and gear, it came to him—the way the monk always carried the bamboo case with him, the way he never let it out of his sight. The way he'd slept with it in his arms. The way he'd come after Kar the instant he'd realized it was missing.

The case now fastened to his shoulder, the monk motioned for Kar to step up onto his hands, linked together to provide a step up. From there, he gave Kar a push so powerful that the young thief was propelled upward, to a ledge just beneath a blasted-open skylight.

This was not human strength, Kar realized with a shiver. The monk possessed a secret, one he was willing to die for.

The monk scrambled up the corner of the wall as easily as a lizard, then moved with perfect balance over to the skylight.

And he opened the bamboo case and handed Kar the Something that everyone was so desperate for, the thing that Kar, in his ignorance, had stolen, thinking it was a cheap little piece of Hong Kong paraphernalia to be pawned for quick cash: the scroll.

"Hold this and stay out of sight," the monk admonished him.

And with that, the monk—in another feat of inhuman agility and strength—leaped up through the open skylight.

Kar watched from his perch as the monk scrambled out onto the roof and began to run. Behind him, rising like a dark sun, the helicopter maneuvered into position. Kar peeked up over the edge of the skylight, feeling utterly helpless to protect his friend.

The helicopter was equipped with a machine gun—and as Kar watched, it sailed over the monk, then lowered itself in front of him, blocking his path.

The Suits were going to mow him down, and there was nothing Kar could do about it.

His attention was at once drawn to the stairwell opening on the roof behind the monk; with a shattering of wood, its door burst open, and two more Dark Suits ran out, effectively trapping the monk between them and the helicopter.

One of the Suits smiled, hefted his gun, and aimed it point-blank at the monk.

What happened next occurred in less time than it took the Suit to pull the trigger.

Kar's thoughts raced at light speed. What was it his master had said? You couldn't see the air . . . but it was there, nevertheless, in your lungs. You could walk on it, swim through it. . . .

Kar believed because he *had* to believe. . . . There was no other way to save his friend.

And he went sailing upward from his perch, moving through the air as if it were his ally, outside onto the warehouse rooftop and into the path of the gun-wielding, dark-suited men.

Airborne, Kar kicked out, lightning-fast—faster than he had ever before believed himself able— and knocked the two men down.

Gunfire spilled up and out, going wide around Kar and the monk.

The monk noted his student's act of courage and skill with gratitude—not so much because of the fact that it spared his, the monk's life, but because it confirmed that indeed, Padmasambhava, the beloved Buddha of Tibet, had led him to this young American. Even in the midst of such danger to Kar and to the scroll, the monk felt a blissful happiness: all was unfolding as it ought.

Thus, he faced the helicopter without fear, despite the fact that it was clearly preparing to fire its Gatling guns at him. Rather than flee, the monk dove directly at the helicopter—

—and beneath it, hiding himself from view of both the pilot and the two armed mercenaries on the rooftop.

The helicopter slowly began to rise as the monk clung to its landing skids; carefully, he climbed, balancing all his weight first on one hand, then the other, until he reached the pilot's side of the aircraft, and the open door there.

On the ground below, the mercenaries were still desperately searching for him.

Leaping upward, the monk caught hold of the copter's roof and propelled himself feet first into the craft—

—and landed a hard kick in the chest of an armed, dark-suited man, one of three, in addition to the pilot.

Caught completely off guard, the man flailed his arms, seeking purchase, but the impact of the monk's blow was too great. The mercenary went sailing backward out of the helicopter.

The monk watched him fall some thirty feet to the roof below and crash through one of the few unbroken skylights; all the while, the Tibetan chanted the mantra of Avalokiteshvara—*om mane padme hum*—praying that the mercenary might survive; or, in the event that he did not survive, that the blessed Buddha might lead him safely into the afterlife, and aid him in attaining a better rebirth.

Inside the copter, the dumbfounded pilot motioned for another of the armed men to deal with the monk. By this time, the Brother With No Name once again swung from the helicopter's skids, like an Olympic gymnast on the parallel bars; with each swing, he gained more momentum.

This second mercenary got down on his hands and knees and crawled to the edge of the deck, leaning out the open door; his hair ruffled in the wind kicked up by the altitude and the chopper's blades.

He spotted the monk at once, and hoisted a submachine gun in his arms. But before he could pull the trigger, the monk swung forward, catching his arm and rotating it in an inescapable hold.

The monk heard and felt one of the bones in the man's forearm break. He regretted the suffering he had to cause, but such was his karma. There was no other way.

The mercenary screamed in agony and struggled—which only dislocated the bone further and made his pain worse. Firmly, the monk wrapped his fingers around the struggling man's trigger hand, and forced the machine gun to unload its deadly ammunition into the belly of the aircraft.

Despite the wind roaring in his ears, the monk heard the bullets as they chewed through the helicopter. He could not see with his eyes that the pilot above them was wounded, or that the control panel had been damaged, but he sensed these facts with the internal vision his master had taught him long ago.

Like a great wounded bird, the helicopter began slowly to spin out of control.

The monk chanted silently for the mercenary he had wounded, for the pilot, for the situation, that the outcome would bring the best possibility for enlightenment to all beings. Again, he regretted the suffering he had caused . . . but he knew, too, that destiny demanded it.

As the helicopter continued to spin, the Gatling gun beneath it began to fire wildly, randomly, the spray of bullets chewing up everything in their path—including a large satellite dish poised on the rooftop.

The monk waited patiently for the aircraft to move over a safe spot on the roof . . . then he let go of the skids, and dropped onto the rooftop with feline grace. He watched with only sorrow as the helicopter sputtered, coughed, then weaved unsteadily away, black smoke pouring from its rotor.

Nearby, Kar raced toward him, the scroll in his hand . . . but before the young American could reach the monk, the bullet-riddled satellite dish snapped off its foundation and toppled off the roof. The monk turned, sensing danger: there came a ripping sound as a long length of cable, attached to the dish, rapidly snaked off the roof.

In midstride, Kar set down a foot—and instantly the thick cable wound itself around his ankle and pulled him to the edge of the roof. Wide-eyed, he locked gazes with the monk in the instant before he was pulled over. "Oh . . . *SHIT!*"

Then over he went.

The monk leaped to the roof's edge, flattened himself against the ground, and snatched Kar's hand . . .

. . . but the heavy weight of the satellite dish carried the monk over the edge as well.

Even so, the monk did not despair. With an iron grip, he seized the edge of the roof; with the other hand, he held on to Kar.

They swayed together above the street, hundreds of feet below.

The monk thought only of the blessed power that had flowed through his body on the day his master anointed him the Next. He breathed deeply and let that power surge through him now.

And, trusting in his might—not truly his own, but the might of the buddhas—the monk gritted his teeth and heaved upward with all his might. Slowly, slowly, he pulled himself and Kar—still shaken and wide-eyed—back up toward the roof.

Suddenly, the bamboo case holding the sacred scroll fell from Kar's shoulder, headed for the ground. . . .

But with the skill of a well-trained monk, Kar snatched the case from the air.

Both he and the monk sighed with relief.

And then the case itself suddenly fell open. . . . The sacred scroll fell out, hopelessly beyond Kar's desperate grasp, and sailed down to the street below.

The monk watched, helpless, as a black Mercedes SUV came screeching down that particular street, and stopped directly in front of the scroll.

A woman—young and blond, of Struker's blood, the monk knew—emerged from the driver's side. She raced to the scroll, seized it, leaped back into the car, then drove madly back down the street.

The monk felt a sense of defeat—for only an instant. This loss of the scroll was only temporary; it was his duty and his karma to retrieve it and keep it safe. To permit himself to revel in defeat would only ensure it; thus, he dismissed it.

He gave a final, mighty yank and managed to pull Kar up over the roof's edge. Both of them exchanged exhausted looks.

But Kar was haunted by a sense of failure, one he could not hide from this monk who would be his master. He, Kar, had lost the damned scroll—the only thing the monk had asked him to look after.

All he'd done was cause the monk trouble; it was time for him to leave before he wound up getting the monk killed, as well.

He shook his head grimly. "Sorry about the scroll, man—and thanks for saving my ass—but I just came *this close* to being *killed*. I'm a thief, not a hero—and I'm outta here."

He pulled himself wearily to his feet and turned his back on the monk. The guilt was numbing, but he saw himself as useless now—beyond useless. He made his way over to a fire escape leading down to the street. . . .

"Kar," the monk said.

Kar kept walking. In the distance, police sirens howled.

"Don't you want to know the *truth?*" the monk asked.

Kar stopped. Hesitated. Turned. Then locked eyes with the monk. "Oh, great. *Now* you decide to come clean?!!"

The monk smiled, a big Buddha smile, and closed his eyes as if he hadn't a care in the world . . . as if the building weren't in shambles around them, along with hundreds of bullet casings, as if a huge, shot-up satellite dish weren't hanging by a few cables from the rooftop. As if the police sirens weren't right up on them now. As if they both hadn't very nearly *died*.

"Open your mind," the monk said. "Concentrate on the dreamlike nature of existence."

The sirens stopped. Kar peered over the edge of the roof and counted four police cruisers pulling right up in front of the warehouse. Cops ran out of the cruisers and into the warehouse.

"Are you crazy?" Kar tugged at the immovable monk's arm. "C'mon, we gotta get out of here right now!"

"Shhhh." The monk's smile broadened. "You must let go of everything."

Let go of everything? Kar wanted to shout. *The cops are racing up the stairs for us right now!*

But the monk opened his eyes, and those eyes were infinitely ancient, infinitely compelling. "True forms neither appear nor disappear. So relax . . ."

He raised a hand and pressed a finger against the indentation of Kar's upper lip.

White light. Brilliant light. A power passed through Kar's body that felt like a cleansing breeze.

". . . and simply meet what comes," the monk finished.

The light began to fade; temporarily blinded, Kar blinked until at last, his eyes made sense of his surroundings . . . and he felt as though his heart had caught in his throat.

The warehouse rooftop, the cops, the satellite dish—all of it had completely disappeared. And in its place was a brilliant blue sky, set against snow-capped mountains, glittering like diamonds in the sun.

And he and the monk were balanced on the very apex of one of the highest cliffs; on either side of them was a sheer drop.

Kar experienced a mixture of pure terror and pure awe. "*Holy shit.* How . . . ?"

"We followed the dream," the monk said. "It was on this very mountain that my master first told me about the *Don Dam Pa Mdo*—the Scroll of the Ultimate. Whoever reads its mantra aloud will be blessed with the power to control the Four Elements of Nature—Earth, Wind, Fire, and Water. Man and nature together shall create a perfect paradise."

Kar frowned, trying to understand. "If that scroll really can do all that stuff"—and at the moment, everything the monk had done definitely convinced him it could—"why are you trying to keep it a secret?"

"Because." The monk sighed, and for the first time, Kar saw a troubled look creep into his eyes. "In the wrong hands—that which can bestow peace and prosperity . . . can also wreak chaos and destruction. . . ."

The monk reached inside his jacket and pulled out a cloth, which he unwrapped. It was a mural of sorts, covered with images of people being killed . . . by terrible earthquakes, floods, storms, fires. . . .

Earth, Wind, Fire, and Water, Kar realized. A chill ran down his spine. . . .

"This isn't real," he said. He wasn't so much speaking to the monk as to himself, trying desperately to convince himself that this was all a dream, that he would wake up in his crummy bed in his crummy little room next to the projection booth. Suddenly, that didn't seem like such a bad place to be.

But his own eyes did not deceive him: he was fully conscious, not asleep, still sweating hard from the fear and exertion of being pursued by the men in dark suits, and he was standing beside the monk on what appeared to be a Himalayan mountainside, breathing in the impossibly pure, frigid mountain air, thin because of the great altitude. In the distance, the tallest peaks Kar had ever seen spiraled up into the clouds.

"The power of the scroll is revealed in these pictures," the Brother With No Name said somberly. He was perfectly composed, at ease despite the dizzying height. "It is the reality which my brotherhood has stood guard against through the centuries—and which I stand guard against now. Humanity must be a hundred times closer to enlightenment before we can risk having one word of the scroll being read aloud by anyone."

He again lifted his hand, and pressed Kar in the same spot just beneath his nose.

Another flash of light engulfed Kar . . .

. . . and in the next instant, he stood beside the monk atop the warehouse roof. He could only gape at his master in pure wonder.

At the same time, he heard the cops storming up the stairs. Soon they would be at roof level. But Kar still stared at the monk. "How . . . What did we just—?"

Somehow, the monk understood. "A vision that lasts *hours* in the mind can be *one single moment* back in the physical world." All the concern and

gloom had left his features, and were again replaced by the all-knowing smile. "*Now* we should
go."

The monk headed for the fire escape, and Kar
followed.

By the time the police smashed the rooftop door
wide open, the two of them were gone.

7

The monk dropped the last few feet from the fire escape; Kar followed, hitting the street and racing off with the one he had come to think of as his master. Behind them, a bevy of police cruisers pulled in beside the warehouse, and the scarred satellite dish that hung perilously above the street. A crowd had already started to gather, gasping and pointing at the dish and the shattered skylights on the roof.

Kar's mental activity was no less frantic than his physical. In the midst of a full-out dash down the street, he was still trying to process the last few moments of his life, which had definitely been the most extraordinary: the monk's physical prowess had been nothing less than magical, and the shared vision on a mountaintop in Tibet . . .

Kar tried to hold on to his skeptical life view

and failed utterly. Perhaps there *was* such a thing as destiny, and True Good versus True Evil. Perhaps all the Hong Kong martial-arts movie bullshit about monks with amazing powers was true after all, and there was such a thing as enlightenment.

If so, this nameless monk surely possessed it.

Gasping, Kar called to the monk, "So who are these guys that are after the scroll?"

Opportunity presented itself in the form of a cab coming down the street toward them; Kar did not wait for an answer, but instead hurtled out into the middle of the busy street and waved down the cab.

It screeched to a halt—barely missing Kar. He threw open the door for the monk—who, the instant before he slipped inside, paused to answer Kar's question.

"Mercenaries led by a Nazi—a hungry ghost obsessed by the past."

Kar shuddered at the words *hungry ghost*. He knew only a little bit about Tibetan Buddhism—but enough to have heard about the *bardo*s, the phases a soul supposedly passed through after death. At one point, the soul was confronted by hungry ghosts—desperate souls trapped between life and death, unable to move on because some trauma, something they still clung to from a past life, kept them in limbo. It made Kar think of vampires, trying to steal the very life essence from their victims.

He mentally pushed the disturbing image away

as he hopped into the cab after the monk and slammed the door.

Inside the cab, the monk was grateful for Kar's presence; he felt now that Kar had indeed become his student, and was perhaps even the Next he had been so long awaiting.

At the same time, he noted the cabbie—a turbaned Sikh involved in what the young people today called multitasking: While the Sikh was busy listening to loud sitar music on his radio, he was simultaneously studying a street map and speaking rapid-fire into a cell phone . . . all while pulling away from the curb and speeding out into the city streets.

Clearly, the cabdriver had been deeply affected by his time in America. But the sight of the Sikh brought a rush of pleasant memories for the monk. He smiled, and switching from English to fluent Punjabi, greeted the man in the traditional Sikh manner.

"Never fear—never inflict fear. Downtown, please."

Reflected in the rearview mirror, the driver's eyes brightened at once. In Punjabi, he replied, *"God is true and timeless!"* Then, for the sake of Kar, he shifted to English. "You speak like you were born in the Punjab, my friend! I'd think you were a follower of the Guru's Path yourself, but . . ."

The monk ran a hand through his close-cropped hair and over his clean-shaven face. "I know—not enough hair." Sikh beliefs demanded that men neither cut their hair nor shave their faces; and indeed, the cabdriver's coal black beard was long and curling.

Kar was watching the entire exchange with wide, curious eyes; out of courtesy, the monk turned to him and explained. "In Kashmir, I studied the *Siri Guru Granth Sahib*—the Enlightened Teachings of the Gurus—and *Gatka*, the Sikh martial arts . . . until Struker found me again."

Kar tilted his angular young face—*so young*, the monk thought with affection and regret, *to have to face such evil*. The American had already lived a difficult life on the streets . . . and it was not about to get any easier for him. The monk, at least, had grown up supported and cared for by his "family" of brother monks and his master . . . but Kar had apparently had no one.

"Struker?" Kar asked, but understanding soon followed. "He's the leader?"

The monk nodded. "His dream is to remake the world in his own image. Every race, creed, and color he deems inferior, destroyed." The monk repressed an internal shudder at the thought of a mind so miserable and deluded, so full of self-hatred that it was capable of wanting to harm others. "Total genocide."

Kar's expression went slack with a sudden realization; then his face and body tensed as he turned to the monk in alarm. "*Wait a minute*—you screwed up big time! If all this insanity is even *re-*

motely true, you should've let me die and saved the scroll!"

The monk felt appreciation for his young student's sense of altruism. Kar did his best to pretend he was motivated strictly by selfishness, but of all the people in the Bishop Square subway station, the young man had been the first one to leap into the path of an oncoming subway train in order to save the life of a little girl. Kar might pretend to be hard and uncaring, but his heart was filled with goodness. The corners of the monk's mouth quirked up ever so slightly. "Relax, Kar," he admonished lightly. "I place great value on your life—but not as much as I place on the life of the world."

The monk struggled hard not to smile at Kar's quizzical reaction.

Inside Grandpa Struker's inner sanctum, adjacent to the Human Rights Organization's control room, Nina watched as the aged man held up the scroll in a trembling hand and regarded it with a sense of infinite satisfaction. Nearby, a team of Struker's armed and black-suited bodyguards looked on proudly.

Nina, however, was worried. The scroll—nothing more than an unimpressive roll of white rice paper—was sealed behind a wide iron band with four small, intricate locks inscribed with tiny Tibetan script.

She frowned at her grandfather. "You never said anything about a locking device."

Struker was unruffled. From behind the oxygen mask, he wheezed, "Relax, my dear. Surely you are familiar with the Fourfold Noble Truths of the Buddha. They all revolve around something I am very familiar with indeed . . ."

Nina finished for him—she had familiarized herself with the teachings of Tibetan Buddhism in order to please the old man, even if she found the beliefs disgustingly weak and passive. "Suffering."

Struker graced her with a smile that was more grimace, then squinted at the inscriptions on the lock and began to deftly click and slide each intricate, separate device.

"The Truth of Suffering . . ." he intoned.

Nina knew the teaching. Everyone born into this world learned it soon enough: To be alive was to experience suffering—emotional and physical—and to experience the inevitable slide into old age and death. Looking at the decrepit aged body in the wheelchair beside her, she shuddered at the realization that one day, she, too, would lose all her youth, attractiveness, and strength. Her vision would fail, and her hearing; she might well become sick and die in pain.

Click. The first part of the device sprang into place; Nina let go a sigh of partial relief.

"The Truth of the *Cause of* Suffering . . ."

Grasping. Trying to hold on to everything American culture valued: wealth, power, youth, health, beauty, life . . . it was this part of Buddha's teaching that Nina despised the most. The fact was, all these things were *good*, and to be sought after. Only the weak, who had no hope of ever attaining such things, would follow Buddha's teaching.

Clack. The second part of the device slid into place.

"The Truth of the *Cessation* of Suffering . . ."

The fact that suffering could truly end, which Nina simply did not believe.

Clink. The third part shifted into place.

"The Truth of the *Cessation of the Cause of* Suffering," Struker finished.

By letting go of all grasping, one's suffering ceased, and one became enlightened—and freed from the Wheel of Death and Rebirth to attain the glorious state of nirvana, or Bliss.

Such bullshit. Yet the Tibetans had a source of real power—one that, because of their foolish teachings, they were too stupid to take advantage of.

Clunk. The fourth and final part slipped into place. The iron band popped open; Struker gazed up at his granddaughter, his smile now wide and triumphant. He lifted a frail arm and gestured to her.

She knew what to do; they had spoken together about this event many times, but she could hardly believe now that it was actually taking place. A part of her still did not believe that Struker's tale of incredible power was actually true.

But still, she reminded herself, there *were* sixty years' worth of newspaper clippings. . . .

Nina led a team of technicians in slowly, gingerly removing and unrolling the fragile rice-paper surface of the scroll. Once the delicate paper was unrolled, a technician gently dipped it into a chemical bath.

Nina drew in an amazed breath. Instantly, the words on the scroll began to radiate with power. It was true, then. All Struker had told her was true. . . .

Nearby, the bodyguards shielded their eyes from the blinding glow.

Joyous as a child, Struker leaned forward in his wheelchair and pored carefully over the ancient Tibetan script.

Nina could hardly contain herself. "Well . . . ?"

At last, Struker raised his wrinkled face to hers—his expression dark, deadly with rage.

"It's not the secret of Ultimate Power," he croaked. "It's a Tibetan recipe for *noodle soup.*"

The head bodyguard let go a guffaw—then, realizing his potentially fatal mistake, tried to cover it with a cough.

Struker turned to glare at him, then grabbed a pistol from Nina's holster and aimed it point-blank at the bodyguard's face.

Nina did not breathe—no one in the room did, except Struker. She watched as the old man's finger tightened on the trigger; she tensed, fully expecting the gun to go off any second.

Instead, Struker spoke, his tone deathly quiet. "*You* . . . will cook me a bowl . . . of the *noodle soup.*"

Eyes wide, face frozen in an expression of terri-fied respect, the head bodyguard swallowed hard, then nodded.

Struker swung the gun about, and pointed it di-rectly at Nina. She struggled to keep her fear from showing. He could not know she meant to betray him . . . or could he? She had told no one. . . .

"You may be my granddaughter," Struker warned her, "but that will only protect you for so long."

And again, his finger tensed on the trigger. Nina did not permit herself to tremble. He could not know, she told herself. This was only a test of her loyalty. She lifted her chin, defiant. She would admit to nothing.

Struker seemed pleased by her reaction. With a swift move that startled her, he turned the pistol about so that the butt end faced Nina, then tossed it to her.

She caught it nervously, cursing herself for her fear.

Back in the moving cab, Kar was gaping at the monk over another new revelation. This had, with-out a doubt, been the single strangest day of his life.

"Noodle soup?!" Kar exclaimed, in response to the monk's calm explanation as to why no one need be alarmed over the loss of the scroll. Ap-parently, the piece of rice paper in the bamboo case—so jealously guarded by the monk—had

been nothing more than a distraction to lure enemies away from the truth. "Then where's the
scroll?"

The monk's eyes gleamed with sudden humor,
as if he had just told an enormously funny joke.
"You're looking at it."

Kar shook his head as though he could clear
away his growing confusion. "What?!"

The monk's jacket was open; beneath it, he wore
a collarless cotton shirt, which he pulled down
slightly to reveal skin of pale ocher . . . and something more, tattooed on his chest.

Kar stared in wonder. There, on the monk's
body, was the same sort of sharp, angular calligraphy he had seen on the scroll he'd stolen and tried
to give to Fuktastic . . .

. . . and in an instant, he realized that the Scroll
of the Ultimate had been sitting next to him all this
time in the cab.

"I've been running a long time," the monk admitted. "Too many close calls. The scroll needed to
be someplace safe."

So you created a distraction, Kar finished
silently.

Outside the cab, thunder rumbled in the distance; rain was no doubt on its way.

Kar glanced at the cabdriver—who was fortunately totally distracted by his loud sitar music at
the moment—then lowered his voice. "So you
look, like—thirty-eight? Forty?" At most. "But
you've been protecting this scroll for *sixty years?*"

"Whoever is entrusted with the scroll gains the trust of time," the monk said simply.

Kar stared out the window of the cab as he tried to digest all of this . . . and could not help noticing the swift approach of dark storm clouds. For some reason, they seemed to him an omen of things to come.

In the lobby of the Golden Palace Theatre, Mr. Kojima was still at work behind the concession stand; he was busy cleaning out the popcorn machine when he first took note of the thunder. It must have been going on for some time, he decided, as it seemed very loud and very near. It was going to be quite a storm.

The thunder rumbled again; this time, it was joined by the faintly muffled snap of stiletto heels against the worn carpet.

Kojima looked up—and instantly smiled. A young white woman—very pale and blond, with full, painted ruby lips and large eyes—stood in front of the concession stand. She was impeccably dressed in a fine suit and good jewelry, not at all the Golden Palace's typical customer. In the face of such wealth and beauty, Kojima had no trouble layering on the charm.

"*Hello*, my dear! Welcome to my fine establishment—how can I help you?" He quickly scooped her a bag of popcorn and proffered it to her. "Popcorn? Best in town."

The woman ignored the bag thrust at her; instead, she regarded Kojima with a decidedly icy stare as she flashed an ID card at him. "No thanks. I'm from the Health Department."

So much for charm; Kojima's smile vanished, replaced by a frown. He immediately turned defensive, and pointed to the big blue "A" on the sign posted in the theater window. "Hey, I got an 'A,' see! My place is so clean you could eat off the floor!"

In response, the blond woman gazed coolly down at the floor and squashed a scurrying cockroach beneath the pointed toe of her high-heeled pump. She did so with such obvious pleasure that Kojima shuddered slightly.

In a tone as cold as her eyes, she said, "You have a young man working for you. He *lives* here. You're aware that's a serious violation of health and building codes?"

Kojima glared at her. "I don't know what you're talking about."

The woman gestured toward the doorway, and three men in business suits stepped into the lobby—they'd been waiting, Kojima realized, just outside the door, and now they were closing in on him. With a thrill of fear, he understood exactly what business they were in—and knew that the woman had nothing to do with the Health Department. Kar had gotten himself into trouble before, but *this* was far beyond trouble.

Then one of the pseudo-businessmen pulled out a thirty-five millimeter film can—one of the ones Kar used to store his things in—and slammed it down onto the counter so hard Kojima thought it might crack the glass.

"Does *that* jog your memory?" the woman asked, her voice harsh, deadly.

Kojima's features twisted with fear. He moved swiftly for the telephone—an old-fashioned rotary wall phone nearly as old as the theater itself. If it still worked, Kojima reasoned, there was no point in spending money to replace it. "I'm calling the cops, you crazy bitch!"

With dizzying speed, the blonde seized the old phone from Kojima's hands, pulled the receiver off the hook, leaned forward over the counter, and wrapped the cord around the old man's neck.

He gasped as she pulled the cord, tight.

"I'm not crazy," she said calmly.

Kojima stared at her, eyes bulging, and wheezed as she pulled hard, harder. The curls in the cord disappeared as it grew taut, then at last tore from the wall.

By this time, the old man was dizzy, reeling; his vision was beginning to fade by the time the blonde leaned close to him, and whispered seductively in his ear.

"But I *am* a bitch."

They were the last words Kojima ever heard.

8

Kar and the monk entered the Golden Palace Theatre at dusk; only a few feeble streaks of dying red sunlight managed to filter through ominously thick, charcoal storm clouds. The air was heavy with the scent of impending rain.

Kar dashed first into the lobby, and looked around: empty. No film was playing at present, so the theater was deserted . . . except for one.

"Yo!" Kar called out. "Mr. Kojima?!"

Silence. Maybe the old man was out running an errand—buying more seaweed for the concession stand, or shopping at the Asian grocery store on the corner.

Kar turned to the monk. The Tibetan's expression had shifted ever so slightly from its usual placid Buddha mode to one of concern; the monk's eyes had narrowed ever so slightly. But Kar was so exhausted by the recent events that he chose not to be alarmed by it. Instead, he shrugged. "Well, my boss doesn't seem to be here, which means you don't get to watch me get yelled at. . . ."

He sauntered over to the concession stand and found the Chinese cookie tin where Kojima stored his messages. He popped the tin, dug out the one slip of paper inside, and knew, even before he read it, who it was from.

His eyes lit up at the information. *"Excellent."* He grinned over at the monk and opened his mouth to say something . . .

. . . when his eye caught sight of the wall phone near the soda machine. The smile fled his features at once.

The receiver was missing—and the phone cord, too. Someone had torn it from the wall.

Kar felt suddenly unable to breathe. Ever since the cab ride, when he'd first heard the thunder, he'd been trying hard to ignore the fact that something horrible was about to happen—but now the feeling was unleashed full force. Something had happened to Mr. Kojima, something unthinkable, and he knew that if he finally relaxed and permitted himself to let go his breath, tears would come.

"Son of a bitch," he whispered huskily, then shouted at the top of his lungs. "MR. KOJIMA!"

Instinctively, he raced up the stairs, the monk behind him.

He plowed through the projection room and threw open the door to his tiny apartment.

Inside lay chaos. The movie posters had been torn

from the walls and shredded, his bed overturned, the refrigerator pulled from the wall, its door flung open. Every piece of clothing he owned had been pulled out and flung in a heap onto the floor.

Rain, heavy and diamond-hard, began to pelt the windows.

"Bastards!" Kar yelled. *"BASTARDS!"* This was the work of Struker's Dark Suits, he knew; and he cursed them not for ransacking his apartment— these were only things, after all, which could easily be replaced—but because of the phone cord torn from the wall. Because he could not find Mr. Kojima, and because he knew, with a sickening sense of despair, what must have happened.

The monk stood, quiet in the face of Kar's grief and rage, his expression one of compassion. As Kar struggled with his emotions, the monk carefully surveyed their surroundings . . . then, in a quiet tone laced with regret, spoke.

"Kar. Over here."

Kar heard the monk's words and did not want to turn; did not want to see what he knew the monk had already seen. Yet he turned, and forced himself to look.

Stretched out in a dark corner of the apartment, Mr. Kojima lay on the floor. The old man's mouth gaped open; his eyes bulged in an expression of pure terror.

And wrapped about his neck was the missing telephone cord. Kar knew, without checking, that Kojima had stopped breathing long ago.

"Aw no . . ." he said gently. "No. . . ." A darkness far more profound than that outside overcame him; he felt as though he were sinking into the floor, even though his body somehow managed to continue standing upright.

Kojima had taken him in; had never asked questions even though he certainly must have suspected what his young tenant did for a living. He had harangued Kar like a fishwife, but there had been an unspoken yet honest affection between the two. Kojima had been the closest thing to a father Kar had ever known.

And because of him, the old man had been killed.

Beside Kar, the monk knelt down and gently, respectfully, closed Mr. Kojima's eyes. Then he looked up at Kar. For the first time since the two had met, the monk seemed genuinely shaken.

"I'm sorry, Kar." In his tone was unmistakable, very un-Buddhist guilt. "I should have never gotten you involved. I just . . ."

Kar did not understand. He managed, through some miracle, to speak. The words came out quietly, evenly. "You just what?"

The monk rose and drew in a deep breath. Once again, he shared with Kar a fresh revelation. "I had a crazy notion that maybe you could fulfill a prophecy once told to me by another old man before he died."

Kar stared dully back at the monk. The words made no sense to him; he did not try to think them through. At the moment, he could think only of Kojima's bulging eyes, and the phone cord wrapped about his neck.

After an uncomfortable silence, the monk continued. "They're never going to stop until they get me . . . and the scroll. Go someplace safe and forget about all of this." A ripple of sadness crossed his features. "Good-bye, Kar."

He turned and walked slowly from the room, his shoulders sagging as if beneath a heavy burden. Kar watched him go, and listened to the sound of his footsteps moving down the stairs.

Outside, the rain lashed against the windows. Hardly looking behind him, Kar took a single step backward and planted himself in the one chair that had not been overturned by Struker's men.

For a moment, he sat and thought.

Kojima had died . . . had been murdered by evil men who wanted to seize a power that would wipe out most of the human race. That meant Kar had a choice: He could let the monk walk out of his life, and leave him to fight the evil on his own. He could let Kojima be a simple casualty, let his death be meaningless.

Or he could let Kojima's death inspire him to join the monk, to fight the evil. To make the old man's death count for something. Kojima might have been small and frail, but had he understood what Struker and his men were up to, he would have fought with all his strength against them.

Perhaps he already had.

In his mind, Kar heard Mr. Kojima's voice, and he echoed the old man's words to himself. Kar looked about at the remnants of what he now thought of as his former life: the trashed movie posters, the flipped bed, the clothes strewn about the room. And then he drew in a deep breath and said, with quiet determination:

"Time to fly."

He stood, grabbed some clothes from the floor, and shoved them all in an old knapsack.

Kar raced down the stairs, and charged out of the Golden Palace for the last time.

The rain was coming down in hard, stinging drops, but Kar scarcely felt it; he was too busy looking around the near-deserted street, seeking the monk.

His master had disappeared.

"Shit," Kar swore. *"Shit!"*

He tore down the street, racing to the point of breathlessness, gaze alert for the Brother With No Name. He pulled around a corner—no sign of the monk, so he backtracked and tried a different street, all the while growing more soaked by the second.

Still no monk. Kar spun about, desperately searching. . . .

In the control room, Struker sat alone in his wheelchair, his mask pulled aside, and took another slurping spoonful of the noodle soup made by one of his bodyguards. Struker had indulged in

the faintest of hopes that perhaps the soup somehow conferred strength . . .

. . . but at the moment, he was not only his usual
aching, wheezing self, he was overwhelmed by a
sudden piercing pain in his jaw.

He dropped the spoon back in the bowl with a
loud *clink*, and inserted his fingers into his mouth,
searching with them until at last he found the
source of his misery: a tooth. It moved easily, loose
in its socket, and with sudden ferocity, Struker
yanked it free from the gum.

There came a flash of pain, which ebbed to a
dull ache. Struker pulled the rotten yellowed
tooth from his mouth and studied it with pure
disgust.

The Buddha had been right about the fact of
suffering, and the inevitable decay of the body.
Struker found it an incredible affront and incon-
venience—but he was just as determined that soon
he would find a way around it. He had lived this
long on sheer will, and he would continue to do so,
tooth or no tooth.

He threw the tooth down on the table, set down
the soup, then wheeled himself out to where a
great deal of activity was occurring; his bodyguards and the technicians were busily breaking
open several large wooden crates.

Struker was mightily heartened by what lay inside those crates: gleaming metal machinery, machinery courtesy of much research performed by
the Imperial Japanese Army. Here, the mystical

met the scientific, and Struker could scarcely wait for the results he knew would be forthcoming.

He did not turn at the sound of stiletto heels clacking against the floor; he knew the sound of Nina's movements too well. She was useful to him at the moment, but he trusted her not a whit. Struker's many years on this earth had taught him to be a shrewd judge of character, and he knew well that Nina would betray him the instant she had the opportunity.

His gaze remained locked on the shining machinery. "A new exhibit," he said, smiling inwardly. "Though it won't be open to the public."

Lit from behind by streetlamps, the rain glittered against the night like falling jewels; Kar had run miles in the blackness, and his soaked clothes now clung to him like a second skin.

At the moment, he stood at the door of the pottery factory, which housed the secret temple the monk had led him to. The storefront was dark, but that wasn't about to discourage him: he pounded on the door until his fist began to ache. The memory of Kojima fueled his determination; if he had to kick his way in, he would. But he would never leave.

"Hey! Open up! Somebody—*open the door! OPEN THE GODDAMNED DOOR!*"

He screamed until he was hoarse; at last, a dim light flickered on. Shuffling footsteps sounded behind the door, which at least creaked open slightly.

Behind it, a stocky, white-haired Tibetan woman, her broad face pursed with suspicion, glared out at Kar.

"Excuse me," Kar said, his tone equally polite and desperate. "I'm sorry if I woke you, but—do you remember me? From before? I was with the monk, I have to find him, I—"

The old woman looked him up and down, then countered, her voice flat, "Go away." She began to close the door.

"*NO!*" Kar jammed one foot in the doorway. He had no intention of frightening the lady, but he also would not be turned away. He pushed his way past her, scanning the wooden floor.

At last he found the loose floorboards, immediately dropped to his knees, and began pulling them back.

Just as abruptly, he froze at the feel of cold steel against the flesh of his throat.

The innocent-looking woman and her two elderly friends were now armed with fearsome-looking swords; Kar swallowed hard and felt the blades, razor-sharp, against his Adam's apple. The women's gazes were equally fierce: these were far more than dice-playing little old ladies who ran a pottery factory, Kar realized. These were the guards of the secret temple, and he had no idea what to say to them to keep them from cutting his throat; these women would not be easily charmed.

Fortunately, a voice beside them ordered, "Stop."

Kar looked up and saw Brother Tenzin in his saffron-and-crimson robes.

"He's a friend," Tenzin said.

In the temple's prayer room, the Brother With No Name sat in front of a bowl of steaming water and dipped a cloth into it, then used it to dab at his face. He stared into the small, antique mirror hanging on the wall before him, and studied the reflection there.

In sixty years, it had not changed . . . and, as usual, it bore the fresh marks of his latest encounter with Struker's men. The monk touched a finger to the bruises.

It amazed him that Struker had managed to survive this long; he was by now roughly the same age as the monk—not quite a century old. Strange, how hatred could sustain a body. The monk had always held on to the hope that one day Struker would die . . . and the threat would die with him. But he knew now that was not true. He had learned, through various sources, that Struker had enlisted the help of his granddaughter. The Evil would continue. . . .

And at the moment, the monk was in danger of yielding to hopelessness. He felt old and defeated.

He touched his side and winced, then pulled aside his shirttail, revealing the scar from the bullet wound Struker had inflicted on him so long ago. In his mind, he heard the gunshot, echoing off the infinitely tall Himalayans.

The monk sighed in exhaustion, and let his shoulders sag. He had been running a very long time since that cold morning in 1943.

He tensed slightly at the sound of footsteps behind him . . . but he also knew, from their cadence, that they were those of a friend. He turned, slowly, and beheld Kar. The young man's hair was dark and slicked to his skull from the rain; his clothes were likewise soaked.

A thread of affection wound its way through the monk's exhaustion and despair.

"Hey," Kar said in greeting.

"Hey," the monk said.

For a moment, neither spoke. And then Kar said, his voice quiet but determined, "Listen to me, man. You can't do this alone. You said it yourself, you're tired, desperate—it's been sixty years, for cryin' out loud, you—"

The monk cut him off. "—carry the responsibility of the scroll. On *my* shoulders, no one else's. And if I have to carry it another sixty years, I will." He turned back toward the steaming bowl of water and the mirror. "I'll be safe here till the morning. Then I'm leaving."

"*Bullshit!*" Kar countered. "What about my *training?* You *need* me!"

The monk considered this, and studied the young man with appreciation and regret. Had he never become involved with Kar, the young man's landlord would still be alive. And there was no way to guarantee that Kar himself might not be killed as well.

"I'm sorry, Kar," he said. "But this way is better for both of us."

Kar was immovable; he stood planted in front of the monk. *"No!* You can't leave! You're not abandoning me like this!" Emotion crept into his voice, an emotion laden not only with grief over Mr. Kojima's death, but also with grief over his childhood. "Not after everything you put me through!"

The monk faced him once more; this time, the Brother With No Name had no idea what to say. For the first time, he saw his relationship with Kar from an entirely different perspective. Perhaps it put Kar in physical danger . . . but leaving Kar might be *emotionally* more dangerous to the young man's spiritual path.

The silence between them grew awkward; Kar attempted to speak, choked up, then gained control of himself and said quietly, "Every time I get close to anyone . . . they leave. Go to prison. Or die." He paused. "So now I've got nothing."

He locked gazes with the monk, his pleading.

The monk remained silent a long moment, unsure what to say.

On the sidewalk in front of the pottery factory, four sleek black sedans pulled up and parked. Nina Struker climbed out with a sense of triumph. Through careful investigation of the local Tibetan community—along with some well-placed threats—she had managed to learn of a secret monastery within the city, one she was sure was connected to the monk who guarded the scroll. A little display of gunpower, a little bribery, and she had what she wanted: an insider at the temple, who had contacted her that very evening with news of the monk's arrival. The insider, too, had informed her of the true secret of the Scroll of the Ultimate.

This time, she and Grandpa Struker would not be fooled . . . although she thoroughly intended to rid herself of the old man as soon as she had the monk in her grasp. It wouldn't take much—just the bribing of a few of the bodyguards, and then she would have all the power to herself.

She motioned silently to the bodyguards climbing out of the sedans; together, the group converged on the factory doors—then charged their way in. There were a few old women inside, but the guards shoved their way past and headed straight for the hidden entrance to the temple . . . the one they'd missed the first time they'd pursued the monk into the building.

Nina smiled evilly to herself as the guards pulled aside the floorboards, revealing a staircase leading downward. Soon the scroll himself would be hers. . . .

She hurried down the staircase behind the guards, her heels clacking, and drew in a breath of pure excitement at the sight of the shadowy temple, lit only by the glow of butterlamps and candles, and the golden Buddha on the altar. She had studied such temples, had heard of them, but had never before been inside one, and it seemed to her that the very air within pulsated with diffuse energy. At once, several robed Tibetan monks emerged from the shadows and retreated into a half circle, blocking—Nina noted with keen interest—entry to a small room off the temple proper.

A story that Struker had told her long ago surfaced in her memory: how, high in the Tibetan Himalayas, the monks had formed a semicircle around their small temple, which guarded the Scroll of the Ultimate; how he, Struker, had tried to reason with the monks, to convince them to step aside.

How the monks had refused, and how he had, with a swift, curt downward motion of his hand slicing through the thin, cold air, signaled for his men to shoot.

Nina was not as patient as her grandfather; in her estimation, any time for requests or reason had passed many decades ago.

With the same abrupt chopping motion Struker had used, Nina signaled for the guards to attack.

Back in the prayer room, the monk finally made a decision and parted his lips to say something to Kar—then froze as a sense of imminent danger overtook him. He lifted his eyes overhead, as if to the buddhas . . . but he knew his enemies were already much closer. A sense of knowing told him they had already entered the secret temple; that same sense told him his brother monks already encircled him in an effort to protect the scroll.

"They're here," he said. Déjà vu overtook him. In his mind's eye, he returned to the pristine Tibet of sixty years before, when he stood with his master in the Temple of Sublime Truth and became the Next. In his memory, he heard the echo of machine-gun fire—and saw, all too well, the blank, unseeing stares on the faces of his murdered brothers.

He remembered his master, lying lifeless in his arms.

The sound of flesh pommeling flesh filtered from the other room; there came soft, Tibetan groans, and the harsh grunts of Struker's mercenaries. The monk knew all too well that if the mercenaries did not succeed with their fists, they would not hesitate to use their automatic weapons.

Humanity welled up in the monk's heart, overriding his Buddhist training about karma—if it was the fate of his brother monks to die, then they would die—and detachment. While he had always understood with his mind that he was not to blame for the deaths of his brother monks sixty years before, the monk experienced a resurfacing of long-buried guilt.

He could not permit the same thing to happen again.

Thinking only of the others, wanting only to help, the monk headed for the door to the temple.

Kar immediately stepped into his path. "No."

The monk's expression hardened. "Get out of my way. My brothers—"

"No," Kar repeated, with equal determination. His gaze was oddly calm, placid, filled with deep understanding in the midst of his concern; for an instant, the monk thought, he looked very like one of the brothers. "You have to escape," the American said, every word emphatic. "The *scroll has to escape."*

Beyond them came the sounds of bodies colliding against walls, of shouts, of groans.

The monk beheld Kar with an odd sense that they had just exchanged roles; his student was now his advisor. Yet the monk felt great conflict. "Escape to where? This was my last sanctuary."

Uncertainty glimmered across Kar's features . . . then transformed into triumph. With a sense of accomplishment, he dug into his pocket, then produced a slip of paper. The monk glimpsed feminine writing, an address, a phone number.

"You get us out of here," Kar said, with a confidence the monk did not feel. *"I'll* get us a safe place to crash."

Trying to ignore the cries of pain filtering through the closed door, the monk stared hard at Kar for an instant. In the young man's face, he saw a determination that would not be argued with—a determination he knew filled the heart and mind of each of his guardians fighting for him out in the temple.

They were all willing to sacrifice themselves so the monk could escape.

No, the monk realized, not so *he* could escape.

Kar had spoken well: so the *scroll* could escape. It was that duty that the monk could not permit himself to forget.

And so the monk silently repeated the Vajra Guru mantra to himself—the prayer that the enlightened buddha Padmasambhava would grant him enlightenment and the powers to attain that enlightenment, and to fulfill his karma here on earth.

In an instant, peace and confidence descended upon the monk. This moment of apparent defeat was no more than that: a moment that soon would pass, a dark emotional cloud sailing swiftly against the peaceful blue sky of eternal, unchanging Bliss.

Instinct—or perhaps the wisdom of the buddhas—directed his gaze to the ceiling, where the prayer flag inscribed with the Heart Sutra hung.

In the dim, flickering light cast by the butter-lamps that lined the temple altar, Brother Tenzin stood next to his young protégé, Brother Dilgo, the one he had so hoped would be the Next.

That hope would apparently soon be dashed. All of Tenzin's brother monks had been brutally set upon by the black-clad Americans and now lay—unconscious, dead, or disabled—on the wooden floor. Now, five Americans turned their violent attentions on Tenzin and Dilgo, the last two standing monks, who guarded the door.

Tenzin prayed that they had won the Brother With No Name enough time to escape. He also experienced an insight: he, Tenzin, had been guilty of grasping, of clinging to the notion that *his* protégé would be the one to become the Next. It had driven him to show Brother Dilgo inappropriate favoritism, to reveal certain truths about the scroll that should have been reserved for the Next alone.

As a young monk, Tenzin had listened with awe to the stories told him by his master, Brother Sogyal, who, as a boy, had been witness to the amazing events in 1943 Tibet. Brother Sogyal had witnessed with his own eyes the incredible passage of mystical power to the Brother With No Name as he became the Next; he told, too, of how that brother had miraculously survived a fatal fall from a mountaintop, and a bullet from the German, Colonel Struker, that surely would have killed any other mortal, monk or otherwise.

Listening to the stories, Tenzin had begun to nurture a craving in his heart: he had prayed to the buddhas that *he* might become the Next, blessed with amazing magical powers. And when, over time, it became painfully clear he would never do so, he began to pray that he might at least be the master of the student who became the Next.

Brother Tenzin realized now that he had nursed a small, dark core of jealousy toward the Brother With No Name and the young American, Kar. Had he accepted Kar's presence without that jealousy, Brother Tenzin realized, perhaps he might have sensed the potential in him that the Brother With No Name had.

Now, the Americans approached threateningly—bringing with them the promise of death or, at the very least, great harm. Behind them, the blond woman watched, her full, ruby lips curved upward in a sadistic smile. How very beautiful she was, Tenzin reflected; and how that beauty masked such very great evil.

He turned to his young protégé with words of encouragement.

"Stand fast," he told Dilgo. "We must protect our brother at all cost!"

With admirable calm, Dilgo regarded his master . . . and then the young man's eyes narrowed, and his expression turned inexplicably brutal. He whirled to face Brother Tenzin, then lashed out at him with a series of brutal, lightning-fast blows.

Beneath them, Tenzin sank to his knees in horror—not so much at Brother Dilgo's betrayal, but at his, Tenzin's, blindness to it. His own craving to be the one to find and nurture the Next had led to his inability to sense grave danger to the *Sangha*, the Buddhist community. He looked up at his young protégé, his eyes wide with surprise, and asked a single, simple question.

"Why?"

Brother Dilgo stared down at his master and let go a derisive laugh. "Even if I had been chosen to be the Next, what would it mean? The chance to be chased all over the world until I'm caught or killed or—if I'm lucky—get to pass the scroll on to the next poor fool? I don't want to *protect* the

scroll—I want to *read* it . . . and *take* the power."
Dilgo shot a meaningful glance at the blond
woman, leading Tenzin to understand at once the
betrayal that had taken place. "Even if I have to
share it."

Forgive me, Brother Tenzin said silently to the
Brother With No Name. And to the buddhas, he
prayed as well: *Forgive me, and may I be wiser in
my next life than I am in this one.* For it was quite
possible that his time in this physical incarnation
was growing short.

Tenzin stared up at his protégé as young
Brother Dilgo lifted his arm to deliver the final,
devastating blow. And in the instant before the
blow descended, Tenzin felt a deep sense of gratitude that he had been permitted to see his faults,
and reflect on them; he was grateful, too, that in
this moment he was able to find compassion, not
hatred, for the young monk staring down at him.

And then Brother Dilgo brought down his arm,
so swiftly Brother Tenzin saw only a blur. The pain
was swift and passing, followed by darkness and
silence. . . .

9

Nina graced the twenty-year-old monk with one of her most seductive smiles.

So much for the integrity of Tibetan monks; a bit of flirting, the promise of power, and this one had been willing to throw away his upbringing and religion. She'd heard so much about the humility of Buddhists, but this particular one was filled with an arrogance that matched her own.

Now he stood, tall and thin but puffed up with pride, over the body of his fallen master.

"Thanks for the phone call," Nina said with disarming sweetness. "We lost him at the warehouse, but nobody gets that lucky twice. Where is he?"

The young monk indicated a small door at a far, dark corner of the temple.

Nina nodded to the bodyguards; at once, they ran for the door and crashed through it.

The young monk led the way; Nina followed. . . .

Then looked in fury at the empty room. There was nothing to be found, save for an old knapsack.

Nina made a beeline for it, lifted it, then angrily dumped its contents out onto the floor.

She scowled at what spilled out: Socks. A T-shirt, a pair of worn-out jeans. Junk. Nothing more than junk.

She directed a glare at the young monk, her tone cold and deadly. "Is this your idea of a joke?"

The Tibetan clearly understood that his life was now at risk; desperately, he looked about the room. . . . For several very intense seconds, he was clearly at a loss.

Then he stared up at the ceiling . . . and narrowed his eyes at a large prayer flag hanging overhead. He reached up and pulled down hard on the flag—unfolding a hidden ladder leading upward.

A bit of water from the rain-washed street above splashed into the room, backlit by the light of streetlamps.

Nina's expression became one of stern approval. She would permit this young traitor to live . . . for a short time longer.

Beneath the sewer grating, Kar peered up and around the corner, where three Dark Suits stood watch in front of four black sedans, idling at the curb. The rain had stopped, and, standing on the slick, shining sidewalk beneath a streetlamp, one of the mercs restlessly laid a hand on the weapon hidden just beneath his tailored jacket. Kar thought of the monks left inside with a sense of sadness, but he also knew that he and the nameless monk were doing the right thing by escaping.

It was the scroll's destiny.

Fortunately, the Suits were all too intently focused on the pottery factory to notice anything occurring in the shadows around the corner.

Kar shivered in the cold runoff from the rain; alongside the monk, he pushed the heavy grating until it gave way, then pulled himself up out of the gutter.

Despite the danger, Kar had never felt so fearless, so alive. For the very first time in his life, he was actually doing something that mattered—and he didn't even care if it sounded corny or not. As alone as he had felt his entire life, now he felt as if he had at last found a place where he really belonged: at the monk's side.

He felt—with a surge of distinctly un-Kar-like emotion that tightened his throat—that at last, he had a family. A mission. A purpose.

Beside him, the monk crawled from the gutter; together they stole their way quietly down the night-darkened street.

Outside, the Human Rights Organization Building stood, dark and imposing, locked off from the rest of the outside world; but inside Struker's control room, the world had become a bright, dazzling display of light, technology, and steel.

The old man sat in his wheelchair admiring the

assembled device—a gigantic contraption that filled the room from floor to ceiling. At its center was a vast computer screen displaying a terrain map of the city; on either side were open, human-sized cubicles fitted with restraints, clamps, electrodes, various probes, and needles attached to long fiber-optic filaments.

Flanked by the young Brother Dilgo, Nina, and his bodyguards, Struker watched with pure pleasure and pride as white-coated technicians strapped saffron-robed Tibetans into each cubicle, mounted the electrodes on their skulls, wrists, and ankles, and stabbed needles into their various *chi* energy points.

Once the monks were in place, the technicians retreated to their consoles in order to monitor their proceedings. Nina stepped forward and wheeled Struker to a spot where he could easily see the faces of each captive monk.

Struker gloated freely to himself: Enlightened or not, these monks could not entirely mask their terror.

"Welcome, Brothers of the Fifth Stage of Perfection," he said, with exaggerated jovial warmth, "to my tribute to the unheralded work of Doctor Mengele's Far Eastern counterparts." He paused, acknowledging each experimental participant with a cold, glittering gaze. "I'm going to use your enlightened consciousness to locate the most enlightened one of all. . . ." He half turned over his shoulder toward the technicians behind him. "But first . . . a little *test*."

The technicians worked their consoles; Struker's giant device began to hum with power.

With cruel delight, Struker gave a slight nod to the guards beside him. At once, they seized the traitorous young Brother Dilgo and dragged him to the machine.

"No!" Dilgo shouted, as the guards fastened restraints across his feet, arms, chest. "What are you doing? *We had a deal!"*

Struker smiled indulgently at him, as a grandparent might at the foolish but charming antics of a toddler: the youth's arrogance was so great that—even knowing Struker's beliefs as he did—he had discounted the fact that he belonged to an inferior racial group destined for destruction. Perhaps he imagined he alone, of all his race, would survive. "Did you really think I was going to share Ultimate Power with *you?*"

The machine surged with power: the young monk shrieked, writhing in agony as his body began to glow with an unearthly light. Struker's smile widened; the machine, then, must have been doing its job, tapping into the mental current generated by Brother Dilgo's well-trained brain. Enlightenment, the Buddhists would have called it—but Struker knew it was just another word for power.

With a thrill, he saw the terrain map on the large computer monitor begin to glow . . . and then the entire machine began to glow as well. Brother Dilgo's enlightened consciousness appeared on the monitor, first as waves, then coalesced into a discrete point, like a blip on a sonar screen. It dissolved again, waves seeking other waves, until it contacted another point of enlightened consciousness . . . another discrete blip.

Struker's aged, failing heart filled with joy; only the most extreme weakness held him back in his chair. "The monk," he whispered, and he did not refer to Brother Dilgo or any of the others bound as captives before him, but to the One. . . . "That's *him.* . . ."

His rapturous attention was distracted by young Dilgo's increasingly anguished screams.

The young monk's head distended oddly—bulging first at one temple, then at the other, as if first the skin, then the very skull itself was being forced to expand by an internal pressure. At last, despite the loud hum of the machine, despite the screaming, even Struker, with his failing hearing, could detect the sound of Dilgo's scalp stretching, of the bones in his skull cracking as the monk's head ballooned, expanding beyond all possibility. . . .

At last, the skin separated with a loud *pop*, the skull with a snap. The young monk's head burst open, spewing blood, bits of bone, and brain. The others looked on, transfixed with horror; Struker merely shrugged, then rolled himself over to Dilgo's corpse, sagging limply against its restraints.

"Of course," he mused to himself. "A man who

would betray his brothers would have the weakest will of all." At once his smile returned. Dilgo, so full of life and youth and arrogance, would never have believed that *he* would perish before Struker—or that Struker would survive to regain youth and strength.

Struker turned to his technicians. "But the machine works!" He paused, then gave the order. *"Commence tracking."*

The technicians leaned over their consoles and began fiercely working. Once again, the machine hummed and began to glow; this time, the other monks all began to squirm in silent agony. With childlike delight, Struker directed his attention to the tracking monitor, where waves of consciousness appeared, then coalesced into the one small blip that represented the Brother With No Name. . . .

And this time, the machine kept working.

At the moment, the monk and Kar were on the bow of a tugboat looking out at the dark waters and the glittering, distant city lights. The monk had made the arrangements to board the craft— the Chinese captain spoke no English, but was happy enough to help anyone fluent in his language. Now the monk listened with a sense of remorse and longing to the haunting melody played by the aged first mate on his two-stringed *er hu*.

Kar, being an American and used to comfort, was wrapped in a wool blanket, sipping hot jasmine tea. But the monk had refused all such earthly comfort. How could he be concerned with such things when his brothers of the secret temple had all been either killed or greviously wounded? And this was not the first time he caused his brothers' deaths at the hands of Struker's henchmen. . . .

The monk stared somberly out at the play of the light upon the dark waters; instinctively, he touched the old bullet wound in his side. It always ached when he yielded to his unenlightened nature, and allowed his mind to be filled with doubt or regret. At the moment, regret was foremost in his thoughts.

"You all right, man?" Kar asked beside him.

The monk turned to regard his young friend with affection, then sighed. Good, kind Kar. He was full of more wisdom and compassion than either of them had ever suspected. "You led me to the path I should have chosen, Kar. Thank you." Without Kar, the monk might well have remained . . . and foolishly let the scroll fall into the wrong hands.

Kar studied the monk with concern for a time, then nodded in understanding. "You're welcome," he replied quietly.

Once again, the monk stared out at the dark river. "Life is filled with choices. . . ." Perhaps the music was making him a bit too homesick. Overwhelmed by memories of the past, the monk slipped a locket off his neck, opened the clasp, and handed it to his young friend. Inside was a faded daguerreotype of the only woman the monk had ever loved. He knew her every feature without looking at the picture: knew the fine, straight line of her perfect nose, the prominent slant of her high cheekbones, the depth in her dark eyes.

He shivered slightly at the memory of her long, down-soft hair, falling down onto the bare skin of his chest, at the feel of her lips in the hollow there. . . .

She was no doubt dead by now; but somehow, sharing her with Kar made her come alive again, if only for a short time.

Kar studied her image for a time with a sense of reverence, then looked up. "She's beautiful. Who is she?"

Once again, the monk sighed . . . this time, with pure longing. "Her name is Amra of Gyangze." He could not bring himself to say *was*. "If I hadn't been chosen to give up my name . . . we would have been man and wife."

Kar's eyebrows lifted slightly in surprise as he handed the locket back. "So you two were . . ."

"Yes." The monk shut the locket with a snap, then slipped it around his neck. "In the days of my Old Nature, I was her lover. And then, when the day of my New Nature dawned . . . I wasn't."

A long silence passed between them, one in which the monk indulged himself in more regrets, and absently put a hand to his aching side.

At last, Kar tried to defuse the tension with

humor. He grinned weakly. "Women. Can't live with 'em—can't live without 'em."

The monk smiled, more out of gratitude for Kar's attempt to be funny than at the comment itself. He nodded. "Unless you take a Solemn Vow of Abstinence." He paused, shaking off all self-pity and instead finding much to be grateful for in his current situation. "So—it's no longer customary to call a girl before you show up at her house?" Kar had shown him the message left by Jade, giving her address and telephone number; it both amused and pleased the monk to see the attraction between these two young people.

Kar shrugged, doing his best to be nonchalant, though it fooled the monk not one whit. "It's the middle of the night. Besides, if I called her she might say, 'No way in hell'—but if I show up in *person* she's not gonna say no to my charming face."

The monk shrugged in reply, then focused his gaze intently on Kar's pale eyes. It was in fact a test, of the sort his master used to use when the monk was very young, to test his mental abilities. The monk thought, *Others have said 'no' to your charming face. What makes you think she won't?*

Kar tilted his head, listening as if the monk were actually speaking, then answered aloud, "Because she likes me, man, that's why—"

He broke off, confused by the realization that the monk had never uttered a word. The monk could only smile.

"What the *hell?*" Kar demanded. "Man—were you just talkin' in my head?"

Again, only the smile. This time, the monk thought, *As a matter of fact, I was. And there is much you have to learn about women.*

Kar narrowed his eyes, listening once more. He put his hands to his ears, as if to blot out the noise. "Hold up, hold up—first of all, *get out of my head.* Second of all, I'm not taking *advice* about women from a monk!"

The monk's smile faded slightly as he sighed. At last, he spoke aloud. "I wasn't born a monk. Nobody is."

Nine sat in the front passenger seat of a swift-moving Mercedes SUV, driven by Struker's head bodyguard, Schmidt. Dark-haired and pale-skinned, Schmidt was lean-faced, his expression perennially cold and forbidding. Both sets of his grandparents had fled Germany after the war, and though their grandson had been born in the United States, he had been carefully taught to value the same things Struker revered: racial purity, the ascension of the Aryan race to world leadership, the aggressive purging of inferior ethnic groups.

Yet for all of Schmidt's outward hardness, he had proven amusingly easy for Nina to seduce and bring into her camp. With Schmidt to back her, she now possessed the loyalty of most of her grandfather's guards. They were tired of Struker's harshness, his abuse, his utter refusal to acknowledge the fact that, without his bodyguards, he was nothing but a helpless old man in a wheelchair.

Nina had promised the guards rewards: not only greater respect, but greater financial compensation, and for a few that Nina found especially attractive, certain . . . side benefits.

When the time came, they would all move against Struker.

That time had not yet come, but it was close.

And grower ever closer, Nina realized with a thrill, as she sat staring at the portable computer screen in her lap. Normally, she would have been distracted by Schmidt's arms working the steering wheel, by his hard, defined biceps pulling taut against the fabric of his tailored jacket.

But now Nina's entire focus centered on the laptop screen, and the schematic of the city that glowed brightly against the surrounding darkness.

More specifically, her attention was drawn to a single brilliant *blip*—a blip that, as the Mercedes sped through the night, grew ever and ever closer. . . .

Kar gaped, awestruck, at the vision before him: a vast, imposing mansion set on a rolling estate, sealed off from trespassers by a discouragingly high wrought-iron fence and a row of elaborately landscaped hedges.

Worse, every few feet, rotating security cameras scanned the area—and, just inside the fence, uniformed guards patrolled on foot . . . guards armed with very large, very deadly-looking automatic rifles in their hands.

From the looks of Bad Girl, and the fact that she hung with Fuktastic and his crew, Kar had assumed he'd find her in a run-down apartment much like his own—or at most, a lower-middle-class house she shared with a bunch of roommates. But he had never expected this. . . .

A freaking fortress.

In fact, as Kar and the monk had entered the ritzy neighborhood, Kar had at first thought they'd gotten lost somehow; and then he'd decided Bad Girl had to be playing some sort of elaborate joke on him, getting even for his stealing her necklace. . . .

Yet when Kar remembered the way she'd looked at him the last time they'd met, he knew she would never toy with him that way. Kick his ass, maybe . . . but he knew he could trust her utterly.

Beside him, the monk spoke, his voice once again serene and determined. "Ninety-six Sterling Place. This is it."

Sterling? Kar thought. *More like twenty-four carat . . .*

The monk began to move; Kar followed. Together, they crept stealthily toward the fence, then stopped behind the row of high hedges, crouching all the while to keep from being spotted by the cameras or the guards.

Kar's heart sank. "This place has more guards than the White House. Hiding here for the night? Bad idea. Let's go—"

Firmly, the monk motioned for Kar to stay put. "Where would we be safer than in a house surrounded by guards?"

Kar drew back, considering this; it *did*, in an odd way, make sense. Still, after being chased for two days by people waving guns, he'd developed even more of an aversion to them. He shrugged. "So, how we gonna get in?"

The monk turned toward him with the faintest glimmer of amusement. "Why ask me? *You're* the thief."

Kar fell silent; once again, the Tibetan had a point. After some thought, Kar replied, "Well, the twin pillars of every rip-off are misdirection . . . and speed."

The monk contemplated this for a few seconds, then dropped abruptly to his knees. Kar eyed him curiously as the monk patted the ground . . . then at last picked up a small, flat stone and turned it in his fingers.

"Misdirection . . ." the monk murmured. He rose, smiled brightly at Kar, then cautiously began to move closer to the fence. Kar moved alongside him, keeping an intent watch on the security guards.

Still hidden by the hedges, the monk carefully lifted the stone, held it at eye level, then squinted with one eye at a distant spot. Suddenly, he hurled it across the rolling grounds.

It struck the wrought-iron fence on the far side

of the estate, with such force that it ricocheted off several bars with a series of earsplitting clangs.

The guards exchanged looks, then headed off to investigate.

The monk gestured for Kar to remain motionless. As soon as a nearby security camera aimed itself in the opposite direction, the monk murmured to himself again.

"And speed . . ."

Suddenly, he raced for the iron fence, and—as Kar watched in amazement—ran *up* its side, then leaped into the air and landed, one foot atop the iron post that anchored the gate.

Perfectly balanced, the monk gestured again to Kar: *Move, now!* Kar sped toward the fence at the same instant the monk whipped off his overcoat. Twisting it like a rope, he slung one end down toward Kar.

Kar grabbed the coat, and suddenly felt himself sailing through the cold night air as the monk pulled him—up and over the fence, then down again on the other side and the rolling lawn. Kar stood on the soft grass and watched the monk jump down and land lightly beside him.

At once, Kar froze at the sound of a vicious snarl emerging from the darkness.

A black and tan Doberman, shock collar strapped to its neck, slunk out from the shadows, its jowls drawn back tautly to reveal shining, sharp teeth.

Nice doggie, Kar almost said, but in truth, there was nothing nice about this particular animal. It stood, still emitting that low, dangerous *your-days-are-numbered* growl, the hackles raised on its shoulders and back, its ears flattened. It was prepared to tear both men apart at the slightest provocation, Kar realized, yet his next impulse was to offer the back of his hand for the dog to sniff, a gesture of friendship.

The monk seemed to read Kar's mind. "Don't move," he whispered.

For an instant—no more—Kar obeyed. In the next second, however, inspiration seized him as he remembered the hot dog stuffed in the cargo pocket of his pants, in what seemed like an eternity ago.

Kar let a hand creep slowly, tentatively down toward his pocket; then, in a flash of his best pickpocket sleight of hand, he pulled out the hot dog and tossed it at the Dobie.

For a terrible moment, the dog crouched as it prepared to strike at Kar . . .

. . . and then it shut its mouth. Sniffed the air. Located the hot dog and began wolfing it down.

As they began to make tracks, Kar grinned over at the monk. "And you said hot dogs were bad for you."

10

Out of sight of the guards and the cameras, the monk and his young protégé made their way quietly around the back of the vast house—the largest house, in fact, that the monk had ever been so close to. Despite its great ornateness and external beauty, the monk sensed deep sadness emanating from it. This house, the beautifully tended trees, bushes, and flowers . . . even the handsome courtyard with its statues and fountain, all had been accumulated with ill-gotten wealth. It was a shrine to Self, to all that was impermanent and meaningless, to all that would fade.

Yet in this house, the monk sensed also a great jewel . . . the heart that resided in the one Kar called Bad Girl. She was here, a beacon of shining goodness hidden by the veil of negativity that radiated from the house and the possessions.

Young Kar was sizing up possible entryways

into the house—back doors and windows—with a thief's studious professionalism. "Everything's locked and alarmed," he said.

The monk nudged him gently, then pointed to a second-floor window, agleam with light from the full moon . . . and ever so slightly ajar. Twenty feet up, the monk calculated.

Kar looked at his mentor. "How 'bout a boost."

At first, the monk almost complied . . . and then a sudden conviction seized him, one he knew not to ignore, for it had come directly from his Buddha-nature. It was time for him to teach his student self-confidence.

"How 'bout you do this one on your *own*," the monk countered.

Kar looked at his master as though the suggestion were completely insane; then his eyes narrowed with disgust. Yet, the monk noted with amusement, Kar at last drew in a deep breath to prepare himself, then stared back up at the window.

"Okayyyy . . ." Kar said to himself, in a less-than-assured tone. "Forget everything you've ever learned about how the universe operates. I can step on the air like a stone, swim through it like the sea. All I gotta do is believe. . . ."

Once again, he drew in another breath, then got a running start, jumped, and began to run up the side of the house's stone wall. . . .

The monk watched Kar's uncertain expression turn to one of complete fear and disbelief. Immediately, the young man's feet slipped out from beneath him; his arms thrashed as he fell heavily onto the ground below.

The monk felt an urge toward pity—but he remembered also how his master had taught in a style both merciless and compassionate. Instead of rushing to Kar's side and commiserating with him over his pain, the monk remained detached and instead looked about to ensure that no guards had heard the sound of the fall.

None had.

Uncertain and wobbling, Kar regained his feet, all the while glaring over at the monk. The young man's ego craved pity and help—two things the monk knew he must not now provide. Kar's ego needed to be curbed, and his heart needed to learn that his body and mind were together capable of the impossible.

The monk shrugged off Kar's glare, and instead gestured for him to head up the wall again.

Once more, Kar backed away from the house, took another running start . . . and this time made it higher up the wall.

Once again, when he realized how far up he had gone, a look of disbelief crossed his features; his feet gave way beneath him again, and he began to fall.

Then an expression of pure determination replaced all uncertainty; in the last instant before he fell, he reached out with both hands and seized the windowsill.

The monk smiled broadly up at his dangling student. Kar's determination had been based in the ego as well, but such determination was of great use in the search for enlightenment. It would serve Kar well. "Not bad," the monk told the young man softly.

The bedroom was unlit save for the single sliver of moonlight admitted by the window. Kar slipped in, keeping his footsteps stealthy and silent, trying to keep his fear that he would encounter someone other than Bad Girl in check.

But the bed was unoccupied, still made, with a decidedly feminine lace-edged comforter and pillows. Kar's instinct told him this room had to be Bad Girl's; it was as though he could sense her presence here, even though the room was empty. Quietly, he indulged his curiosity and began checking the place out.

Over on a bureau sat a old photograph: a woman who looked eerily like Bad Girl, only a decade or so older, and decked out in 1980s clothing and shaggy hair. Beside the framed photo was a letter on Harvard University stationery; Kar picked it up and squinted at it in the dim light.

It was an acceptance letter to Harvard Law.

And *this* chick was hanging out with Fuktastic's crew? What the hell kind of double life was she leading? He glanced up at the row of golden trophies gleaming on a nearby mantel. All from martial-arts competitions, apparently. He drew closer to see if he could read any of the inscriptions. . . .

And nearly fell backward as, backlit by infrared light, a cobra struck out at his face.

It took all Kar's willpower not to scream; fortunately, there came a slight *clink* as the snake's fangs struck glass.

Holy shit, Kar thought, and released a shaky sigh. The deadly creature was encased in a terrarium . . . though why anyone would ever want to keep a cobra as a pet, he couldn't fathom.

But it seemed like something Bad Girl would do, just for the hell of it.

He recovered his nerve and looked about to find an entire collection of terrariums: more snakes, along with several praying mantises. Curioser and curioser. . . .

At last, he made his way out of the room and let his intuition lead him down a vast, carpeted spiral staircase with an ornate gilded banister.

His instincts proved right. In a living room as large as the entire Golden Palace Theatre, in front of a roaring fireplace half the size of Kar's apartment, Bad Girl lay sleeping on a leather couch.

For a moment, Kar could do nothing more than watch her: her beauty held him, mesmerized him. Lit by the fire's glow, her skin seemed incandescent, unearthly, perfect; her delicate auburn brows were furrowed slightly in sleep, her full lips slightly parted. Her sunset-colored hair fanned over her shoulders onto the couch, making Kar long to touch it, to stroke it. He felt a sudden over-whelming tenderness, a desire to protect her, even if it meant his life.

And he knew, just as he had known in a moment of revelation with the monk, that she, too, was destined to be a part of the family he had always sought.

Gently, he nudged her shoulder.

Nothing.

He leaned down and whispered in her ear. "Hey . . . Bad Girl . . ."

She sighed, then released a deep yawn; her eyes rolled open, glazed by surprise and sleep. In an instant of confusion, she looked up at Kar without really seeing him. . . .

He put his hands up to block any blows, but failed to move out of the way in time. In an instant, she had clutched him by the throat, then flung him hard onto the floor. In the next second, she had leaped up from the couch and jammed a foot against his throat.

Kar wheezed, fighting for breath.

She blinked, stared down at him again . . . and at last, thank God, recognized him.

"*KAR?!* What the hell are you doing here?!!"

Unable to speak because of the foot pressing against his vocal cords, Kar pulled the green neck-lace from his pocket and held it up.

The tension drained from her; her muscles abruptly relaxed, and she removed the foot resting on Kar's neck. He sat up gratefully and coughed.

"Where'd you find it?" Bad Girl asked, gesturing with a dimpled chin at the necklace. She reached for it.

Kar yanked it away and held it just beyond her reach. "Not so fast. First we have to settle what *I* get out of this deal."

Her eyes widened with rage. She stared hard at Kar, then at the necklace, then back at Kar again.

She spoke, and her tone was cold. "You're a pickpocket. I didn't *lose* my necklace. You *stole* it, didn't you?"

Busted, Kar thought, and for the first time in his life, staring into Bad Girl's piercing eyes, he could not think of a word to say.

Hidden in the bushes behind the house, the monk permitted himself a moment of bliss: meditation in the lotus position, eyes not quite shut, mind as free and silent as the open night sky.

In such a state, his senses were naturally heightened; and he felt the gentlest of all breezes, cool and soft, against the skin of his face.

Normally, he would not have emerged from meditation for anything but an emergency; but in this instance, his Buddha-nature told him he was about to receive a sign.

He lifted his eyelids. And smiled at the beautiful butterfly settled on a flower beside him.

The moment of transformation would soon arrive. It would not be long now before the transformation of the Next.

Tenderly, the monk coaxed the butterfly onto his finger and studied it. It would be good to cease running. For an instant, he indulged himself in memories, his smile widening as he recalled the snow-kissed mountains of his homeland, so high they reached Heaven; he had not known, until he had left Tibet, that not all countries had peaks ascending far into the clouds. He remembered, too, the wisdom and kindness of his master, and the fellowship he had been lucky enough to share with his brother monks.

These had all been passing forms; his master was now with the buddhas, enjoying the endless bliss of nirvana, and perhaps some of his brother monks were with him. Soon he, the monk, would also pass from this earth, and perhaps soon find release from the Wheel of Life and Death.

But inside the house, the monk knew, the adventure toward enlightenment was just beginning for two young souls. . . .

Bad Girl began to circle Kar—not a good sign, he realized. He'd pissed her off so badly that she was preparing to do what she'd threatened to the first time they'd met—kick his ass.

"You did steal it, didn't you?" she demanded, her voice shaking with rage. *"Didn't you?"*

Kar did his best to sound defensive. "No! Of course not. What kind of guy do you think I am?"

She made a disgusted clicking sound with her tongue. "You can't lie for shit."

"That's not true!" Kar countered, with honest anger. "I'm a terrific liar!" And then he nearly hit himself for his own stupidity. "Anyway, I'm not lyin'—I mean . . . maybe . . ."

She stared him down, implacable, furious. Beneath the heat of her gaze, he felt himself beginning to melt.

"Okay," he said, changing his tone. "Look, clearly we're getting off on the wrong foot here. Let me be honest—I *did* take it, but . . . I wasn't stealing. I was just . . ." He hesitated, realizing he was simply digging the trench deeper. "Borrowin'. So I could . . . give it back." He paused. "Look . . . it was a stupid thing to do. Sometimes I can be kind of . . ."

She helped him out. "An *ASSHOLE?*"

Now, *that* stung. A sudden anger overtook Kar, one that sprang from the memory of growing up on the streets, struggling to find the next meal. *"Hey,"* he said, "I may have lied about the necklace but I never lied to you about who I am."

She bristled. "You're saying *I* did?"

"Uh, *yeah!* Look at this place"—Kar made a sweeping gesture—"look at *you!* I thought you were from the streets like me—but turns out you're just some spoiled rich girl hangin' with some street crew by night, then running home to the lap of luxury by day!"

Her voice grew low and ugly; he had definitely hit a nerve. "So you think you know everything about me, huh? Well, I'll tell you something you don't know: I have twenty-six trophies up in my room and each one is for kicking a different guy's ass!"

Like a cobra, she lunged for her necklace. Just as swiftly, Kar dodged her, and the two of them launched into a dance, circling each other. Bad Girl struck out, arms slicing through the air; Kar countered blow for blow, never letting the necklace fall from his clenched fist.

"You think you're tough?" he taunted. It'd been a long time since he felt this way—not since he was a child, abandoned by his parents, that he'd experienced so much love mixed with anger. "Must be real tough growin' up in this place, huh?"

Bingo; another clean shot, right between the eyes. He watched her wince, then grow even more furious. *"You don't know a damn thing about it!"*

All the while, the two kept up the constant dance, the constant duel; Bad Girl kept striking out, trying to seize her necklace, and Kar kept eluding her.

And in the midst of his anger, the truth came pouring out of Kar as it never had before. "I know I came here because I thought maybe I could trust you. That monk? He's not really my bodyguard— I'm protecting *him* 'cause he's got these mystical words tattooed on his body that some psycho from World War Two needs in order to take over the whole goddamned world!"

At that instant, Jade almost paused in her attack—then figured she'd best keep moving, because what Kar had just said was clearly the most outrageous lie in the entire world, and obviously a ploy to unsettle her so he could move in for the kill.

Still, she shot him a look of pure disbelief. "Are you on crack?"

That so insulted him that it caught *him* off guard. He stopped in his tracks, opened his mouth to make an angry retort . . . and Jade took full advantage.

She grabbed him by an arm, flipped him over her shoulder, and sent him down, hard, on an uncarpeted section of the slate floor.

Triumphant, she knelt down beside him and swiped her necklace from his hand.

His limp, half-open hand.

Jade looked down at his face—pale and clammy, eyes closed, mouth open. In an instant of terror, she quickly checked his pulse.

It was there, nice and strong. But he was out cold, and that filled her with foreboding. She'd once inadvertently given a guy such a bad concussion, he'd had to stay three days in the hospital, and she was terrified now that she'd done some serious damage.

"Oh, shit!" She gently nudged his shoulder. "Kar . . . ?" She bent down close to his ear. "Kar, are you okay . . . ?"

"He'll be fine," a deep, calm voice said behind her.

She whirled about. At the foot of the spiral staircase sat the Tibetan monk, the one Kar had called his "bodyguard."

"*You?!*" Jade exclaimed in surprise. "What are you doing here?"

The Tibetan angled his face slightly, the firelight playing on his features. "That isn't the question you need to ask." He rose and walked with measured steps toward her; as he did, he gestured at the trappings of wealth surrounding them both. "Instead you should be asking yourself why you run away from this palace every night . . . then race back to it each morning."

Jade felt a surge of anger; at the same time, she sensed that this man said these things only because he wished her the greatest good. "Look," she said, managing to speak in an even tone, "with all due respect—I don't really know *you*, you don't really know *me*, so please don't tell me how to live my life, okay?"

The monk shrugged, clearly taking no offense . . . but also not willing to take Jade off the hook, either. "I'm not telling you how to live your life. I'm suggesting you would be happier living one complete life—instead of *two* lives that are *incomplete*." He paused. "Of course, these are issues of Internal Style. Your *External* Style has great integrity. You don't often see Cobra and Mantis techniques so well combined."

She eyed him curiously, taken aback by the compliment, while still stung by his statement that she led two incomplete lives. The comment was all the more difficult to hear since Jade could not deny, even to herself, that it was true. "Thanks," she told the monk. "I think."

Beside her, a weak groan emanated from the floor. She looked down to see Kar's eyes fluttering open. He grimaced and touched his forehead gingerly as if to make sure it was still there.

Jade placed a tender hand on his shoulder. "Kar," she asked, her tone soft and filled with apology, "can you stand up?"

"Uhhh . . ." Kar's eyes rolled back in his head for an instant; his lids flickered, and then his eyes opened again and became clearer. Even so, he made no attempt to shift his position or rise. *Damn,* Jade thought, *don't tell me I've crippled him. . . .* At last, Kar answered weakly. "I thought I *was* standing up."

Jade felt a wave of shame pass over her. She had trained her body to be a weapon, one capable of inflicting death, and she had always known she had a solemn responsibility never to use her power in anger. Showing off to win respect was quite another thing, of course. But Kar had provoked in her such deep emotion that she had forgotten herself, had allowed herself to strike out with more force than was appropriate.

And if she had hurt him seriously, she would never forgive herself.

Fortunately, at that point, Kar began to stir, and with a fresh groan, pushed himself up into a sitting position; his legs moved slightly, causing Jade to relax. *Okay, so he's not paralyzed, thank God. . . .* She leaned in to study his pupils: they were nice and even, showing no sign of concussion. She almost sighed with relief.

Instead, she said humbly, "Look . . . I'm sorry—but you really pissed me off with that 'spoiled rich girl' line."

Kar massaged the back of his head, then tilted it from side to side in order to stretch his neck. His expression and tone were free of anger as he countered, "Well, what am I supposed to think? This house, those guards . . ."

Jade drew in a deep breath, then hesitated. She had not shared the true circumstances of her life with anyone . . . but at last she spoke, sensing that she could trust both Kar and the Tibetan monk utterly.

"Look," she said finally, "my life's complicated. I haven't seen my mom since I was four years old . . . and my dad's Ivan Kerensky." She paused. "Maybe you've heard of him?"

From Kar's gape-mouthed reaction, it was clear he had. " 'Ivan the Terrible'? *Czar of the entire East Coast Russian mob!?!?*"

Miserable, Jade nodded her head, wishing, as she had her entire life, that she had been free to choose her own father. Quietly, she replied, *"Alleged* czar."

Awestruck, Kar stared at her. There was no derision in his gaze, no attempt to mock, just an endearingly childlike amazement. "Unbelievable! *You're a*

Russian mafia princess! So lemme guess—your real name's *Natasha* or *Katerina*—or—"

"My name's *Jade*," she corrected him. It was the name her mother had given her, a name she treasured as much as her necklace, another reminder of vague childhood memories of her mother's love and goodness.

She continued, her tone still quiet; the admission about her father had been more painful for her than Kar would ever realize. "My dad's serving twenty years in federal prison, and people *still* give me whatever I want just because they're afraid of him. That's why I'm running on the street, keeping everything about myself secret . . ." She paused to lock gazes with the monk. "Because that's the one place where I can earn my *own* respect."

The monk had watched the exchange between the woman he now knew as Jade and the young man Kar with a growing sense of anticipation.

And the more Jade Kerensky spoke, the more the monk began to experience the tingling vibration of power in his own body, accompanied by a deep and sure sense of *knowing*. This was his Buddha-nature awakening fully, and it was never wrong.

He was in the presence of the Next. There could be no more doubt.

Unable to mask the amazement he felt, the monk spoke aloud to himself, his voice hoarse with emotion. The words he repeated were ones he had heard many times before from the lips of his beloved master, the words of an ancient prophecy.

"He will battle for love in a palace of *jade* . . ."

The two young people shot him quizzical looks.

"Two out of three," the monk whispered.

Brow furrowed with confusion, Kar angled his head. "Two out of three *what?*"

"Prophecies," the monk answered. He opened his mouth again, intending to further explain—but his Buddha-nature now alerted him to a much more sinister fact.

Evil was upon them; the enemy was about to enter the room.

The monk opened his instincts to his True Nature, and allowed them to direct his next, lightning-swift actions.

He took hold of Kar and Jade and hurled them, full-force, across the room. *"LOOK OUT!"* he warned them, so they would remain out of danger's way.

But there was no time for the monk to do so himself; and this, he realized, was the universe unfolding as it should. He felt no regret.

The window behind him shattered into a thousand pieces of gleaming, firelit glass—broken by grenades that clattered to the dark slate floor behind the monk.

They exploded, sending out concussive waves that threw the stunned monk to the floor. Only by the resolve of enlightened will did he manage to remain conscious.

But try as he might, he could not manage to pull himself swiftly to his feet—which proved to be his undoing.

In the next instant, something cold and sharp stung his neck; instinctively, he reached out and felt the dart, then turned to see who had fired it.

And in the millisecond before he fell, the monk glimpsed Nina Struker, the colonel's granddaughter, standing with a stun gun in her raised hand, a smile of cold triumph on her porcelain, painted face.

Then the tranquilizer took effect, and her beautiful, evil image faded into darkness.

11

Lying on the floor pressed against Kar, Jade stared out from behind the loveseat that hid them from view of the intruders who had used stun grenades to break their way into the house. There were four bodyguards, armed with automatic pistols, and a blond woman, her hair pulled back tautly from her face, her lips as painted and scarlet as a kewpie doll's.

The blonde leaned over the unconscious monk's body. *If she does anything to hurt him*, Jade thought, *I'll have to kill her. Even if it means the bodyguards shoot me down.* She realized that her own guards, who'd been patrolling the estate grounds, were now either dead or unconscious.

But the blonde was gentle, admiring. She crouched down beside the monk, sitting on her high-heeled haunches, and examined his chest. Something she saw there made her pull the monk's shirt aside.

Even in the firelight, Jade managed to see them: tattoos, of ancient Tibetan script. She couldn't make out what the tattoos said, though.

"Clever," the blonde said. She motioned to the bodyguards to lift the monk's body. They complied, and one of them busied himself fastening restraints around the monk's wrists and feet, so that when he finally came to, he would be unable to fight. The guard pulled one of the restraints far too tight; Jade tensed, until the blonde admonished him.

"Be careful with that body of his—it's priceless."

The guard took the hint and loosened the restraint slightly.

As for Jade, she watched the proceedings infinitely stunned. What Kar had said to her—about his protecting the monk because he had "mystical words" on his body, that a psycho was trying to take over the world—wasn't just something he'd made up in order to distract her during their little duel.

Which meant that the odd sense she'd felt when she first met Kar—and then, the monk—had real meaning. She had felt closer to them than she ever had her own family, as if they were blood; as if Kar were her twin. She had known, with that strange insight meditation brought her, that they were destined to have a profound impact on her destiny.

Jade was stunned for a second reason: she recognized the blond woman, yet in the surrealness of the moment, her brain would not function, would not identify this familiar intruder.

Yet as she watched the blonde and the body-guards carry the monk from her house, Jade *knew* she had seen this woman before. Seen her, and felt a chill of pure evil.

She and Kar stayed hidden behind the loveseat, neither of them scarcely daring to breathe—until at last, they heard the slam of the front door.

Jade raced to a shattered window, Kar close beside her. She peered beyond the broken edges of the glass, down at the front lawn, where the group hurried with the monk toward the front gate. Her own guards were nowhere to be seen: she was sick with worry that they were seriously hurt, or dead. At the same time, she realized that her first loyalty—how very odd to feel such profound loyalty to someone who was very nearly a stranger—lay with the monk.

With Kar next to her, Jade watched as the group made their way through the gate, then saw the distant lights of dark sedans as they sped away.

She turned. Kar had already moved a few steps from the window and, as he took in the destruction surrounding them, slumped to his knees in a gesture of unalloyed defeat.

Jade looked down at him, her heart torn by the sight of his suffering. She had been deeply shaken by what had happened—but she also experienced a sudden conviction that she was here, now, for a purpose.

She spoke to him, her voice quiet. "Everything you told me . . . it's *true,* isn't it?"

Kar glanced over his shoulder at her with eyes deadened by grief.

A strange thought entered Jade's brain, as if she were listening to someone else speak, someone much older and much wiser. *He is trapped in his past. He remembers all those he has lost in life, and now he sees this temporary setback as permanent. He believes he has lost the monk forever. He is mistaken.*

And it was Jade's job to return his confidence to him. She filled her lungs with air, forcing herself to be cheerful, and slapped him on the shoulder. "C'mon."

He looked at her, dazed. "What?"

"We need to get *moving*," Jade said. Her mind was beginning to clear, and suddenly she knew exactly where to go: she remembered where she had seen the blonde before.

Kar's features spasmed with a sudden pain that he forced himself to control. He wanted to cry, Jade understood, but instead he turned his latent tears to anger. "Don't you get it?" he demanded. "They got him—they got the scroll—and there's not a damn thing we can do about it." He shook his head and lifted hands to his face. "And it's all our fault—'cause he was too busy saving us to cover his own ass."

Jade countered his sorrow with hard determination. "Well, if he hadn't saved *us*, we couldn't go save *him*."

He stared at her as if she had lost her mind.

"And just how the hell are we supposed to do that?"

Jade fixed her gaze on him, as if somehow, through a mere look, she could transfer some of the strength she suddenly found in her own heart to him. "By going to the Human Rights Organization Building, downtown. The chick who just wrecked my house? She's the executive director of the place."

Kar tried to wave her off, tried to turn back to his despair. "Excuse me?"

Jade crouched down beside him and took his shoulders. She *would not* let him give up. There was work to be done, and they were the only two in the world who could do it. "I was there this morning for an exhibit opening."

"So?" Kar said, his tone infinitely weary.

"So . . ." Jade said. "My dad always told me the best place to hide is the *last* place they'd expect—and the Human Rights Organization is the last place *anyone* would ever expect to find the biggest human rights abusers in history."

Kar lifted his chin ever so slightly; Jade saw hope creep back into his eyes, and very nearly kissed him for joy.

In the mansion's vast garage, Kar watched as Jade pulled away a tarp to reveal a gleaming, armor-plated Suburban.

She had lifted him up from the deepest despair, the worst grief he had ever known: when the monk was taken away by the Dark Suits, Kar felt as though he had lost a father . . . again. Only *this* father had only shown him kindness and compassion; this father had shown him that life could have meaning, that one's actions could be directed by a sense of purpose. That life was not simply an excuse for ripping other people off.

Only this time, Kar had abandoned this second father, instead of the other way around. He'd been paralyzed by guilt.

If only I had attacked the Suits, instead of hiding like a coward . . .

But Jade had a point. The Suits had been packing major weaponry. If Kar had attacked, he'd now be dead, and the monk would be no better off.

This way, they could find him, save him.

And Kar knew, with the most certainty he'd ever had in his short life, that he would never abandon Jade . . . and she would never abandon him. He had a family, and right now he and Jade were on their way to rescue one of its members.

All these thoughts passed through Kar's mind as he stood, once again amazed by something Jade had shown him. Maybe the Suits had assault weapons . . . but damned if Jade didn't have an assault *vehicle*.

She smiled impishly at him. "So . . . how do you like my armor-plated car . . . Kar?"

Filled once more with hope and definitely smitten, Kar could only grin at her. She was definitely hard-core all the way.

He held on to his seat as Jade turned on the ignition, then hit the gas; the Suburban roared out of the garage, down the driveway, and onto the street, all at top speed.

They drove a time in intense silence, Jade weaving in and out of traffic as expertly as she moved her own body performing martial arts. Kar could only wonder how the two of them could possibly save the monk in Struker's very headquarters, no doubt teeming with Dark Suits with even *more* weaponry at their disposal. If they'd been unable to stop a handful of Suits from taking the monk in the first place, how could they ever hope . . . ?

He censored the rest of the thought. Instead, he forced himself to think of the magical experience of standing beside the monk on a Himalayan mountaintop, of shivering in the cool air beneath the bright sun. He remembered the monk urging him to leap for Jade's window—knowing, in his rational mind, that he could never possibly make the jump.

Yet he had made it. All he had to do now was believe.

Beside him, Jade spoke suddenly, her voice calm and quiet, her gaze still focused on the road. "Never thought in a million years I'd be teaming up with a pickpocket to save a monk with no name."

Kar grinned at her. "Lately, I'm thinking . . . *anything's* possible."

She glanced over at him, and graced him with a

dazzling smile that made him catch his breath. It was only a second, perhaps two, that she took her eyes off the road and looked at Kar—but to him, it was a moment of pure, eternal bliss.

Inside a dark, windowless room, the monk, now naked from the waist up, hung suspended from the ceiling by chains wrapped about his wrists.

He sensed the presence of great evil surrounding him: no doubt, he was captive in the heart of Struker's headquarters. The colonel was somewhere nearby. And more: he sensed the nearness of his brother monks, suffering in great pain.

As for the monk, he remained calm, without fear. Hanging by his wrists produced some physical discomfort, but he had now attained a state of deep relaxation and meditation. He accepted this situation and knew that, like all states, it soon would pass.

The door opened, and a sliver of light illumined the room; there came the *click* of high-heeled boots. The monk slowly opened his eyes to see the blond woman, a steel briefcase in one hand, a scrapbook in the other. She smiled as she approached.

The monk said nothing, merely waited for her to speak—which she did, in a tone of surprising familiarity. "I used to think you were a myth," she told him. "Something he made up to lull me to sleep at night. Then one day he showed me these . . ."

The monk did not need to ask to whom she referred. He knew all too well.

The woman opened the scrapbook reverently, and held it so that the monk could see inside. It was a collection of yellowed newspaper clippings, some of them dating back more than fifty years.

"Ever wonder how he kept finding you all these years?" She lifted the scrapbook higher, so that he could get a better view. "It was those good deeds you felt compelled to perform while you were supposed to be on the run, hiding." She dimpled up at him. "You're such a Goody Two-shoes."

She set the scrapbook down on a nearby counter, then did the same with the steel briefcase. The latter she opened to reveal a laptop computer, hooked up to a portable scanning device. The monk heard a hum and saw the screen fill with light as she powered the computer up.

"My name's Nina, by the way," she said, with a seductiveness both coldhearted and playful. The monk could only think of a cat toying with its battered prey. "You don't have a name, do you? That's kinda sexy."

She picked up the scanning device and began tracing it across the tattoos on the monk's bare torso. The monk watched as the lines of Tibetan script slowly began to appear on the screen of her computer.

"So," she said. "How far down do these go, I wonder?"

And with a flourish, she unfastened the monk's

pants and whipped them off, revealing his naked flesh.

The monk did his best to maintain an enlightened state of mind. This woman could not humiliate him unless he accepted that humiliation. His body was his body, nothing more. There was nothing shameful in it—only in the woman's attempts to embarrass him.

Nina scrutinized his body *very* intently. "Hmmm," she murmured. "*That* far. I guess I'll have to scan it all. Every inch." She shrugged, and shot him another cold little smile. "Oh, well—bit job, but somebody's got to do it."

Slowly, teasingly, she ran the scanner further over the monk's naked body, clearly enjoying his helplessness.

"Tell me," she said, running her tongue over full lips. "If you're a devout follower of the Middle Way and the Fourfold Noble Truths . . . does that mean you're a virgin?"

The monk looked at her sharply. It was as though she had known the one question that would bring him shame. Foolishly, he could not stop himself from answering her. "I was not always . . . as devout as I am now."

Nina seemed delighted by this response. "In that case, I'm guessing . . ." She fished something from the pocket of her suit jacket; as soon as she opened her fist, the monk recognized the object at once: it was the locket containing the picture of his only love, Amra of Gyangze. ". . . this isn't your *mother* or your *sister*." She dangled the locket between them, studying it. "Does the almighty Buddha know his servant fell prey to the desires of the flesh?"

"The Buddha knows my body and my mind," the monk answered humbly.

Playfully, Nina wrapped the locket around her wrist, then leaned forward to whisper in the monk's ear, her breath warm against his skin. "In that case, I envy him." She leaned around to whisper in his other ear. "My grandfather would kill me if he saw me this close to you. He's a psychotic old bastard—believes in separation of the races. Me? I think his politics are for shit—but I do believe in *power*. And you stand in the way of that power."

"Your power is a fiction, Nina," the monk told her. "You can't even control yourself."

Rage flashed in her eyes. "And you think *you* can?"

Obviously, she took his words as a challenge: she took a step back, surveyed him up and down, then—like a beast about to devour its victim—ran her tongue once more over her lips.

Then she moved toward her prey, and enfolded her arms about his shoulders.

The monk shuddered. Her touch was velvet-soft, sensuous. . . . Yet a sense of corruption, of moral decay, of a heart totally devoid of compassion, sickened him at the same time he fought not to become aroused.

She pressed her lips to his—gently at first, then

harder, with shivering passion. He felt the heat of her body against his; this was not purely an act of sadism. She truly desired him.

And his body, being male and thus easily provoked, responded against his will. He strained against his shackles, as if somehow physical movement might distract him; he prayed to Padmasambhava for strength.

But it was too late: Nina drew away, then looked down at his body and smiled.

"I'm glad to see your mind's not the only thing that can expand." She chuckled, mocking him. "Tell me, what would the Buddha say if he could see you now?"

From between gritted teeth, the monk replied, "The Buddha wouldn't be concerned with me."

Nina tilted her head; her tone grew coquettish. "Oh no? Why not?"

Even as he spoke, the monk continued to pray to Padmasambhava, continued to regain control of his senses. "He loves everyone as if they were his only child. Imagine the sorrow of a parent watching their child turn an act of love . . . into an act of evil."

Nina froze; the coy smile, the expression of sadistic triumph fled her face at once, replaced, the monk noted, by something very like shame. Her tone turned hard.

"You're no fun, you know that?"

She glared at him in anger for several seconds, then slowly unwrapped the locket from around her wrist. For an instant, she dangled it before his eyes, as if teasing him with it . . . then dropped it to the floor and crushed it beneath the stiletto heel of her boot.

Inside Fuktastic's subway warehouse hideout, Jade waited for the crew's reaction to Kar's passionate plea for help. She knew that she and Kar alone could not take on the old Nazi and all his henchmen alone—and the only ones she knew she could depend on for help right now were Fuktastic and his crew.

She prayed she wasn't wrong. Tastic's gang were a bunch of petty criminals, true, and capable of violence, true—but at the same time, they had a sense of ethics buried beneath all their toughness. If only she and Kar could penetrate through to that . . .

But so far, things weren't looking good.

Fuktastic wasn't talking; his expression was one of disbelief as he was still trying to digest everything Kar had to say. But Sax, Tastic's second, wasn't buying it for an instant. He screwed up his face and grimaced at Kar and Jade.

" 'Nazis'? 'Scroll of the Ultimate'? You're both talkin' some crazy-ass, whacked-out *bull*shit."

The rest of the crew—all except DV and Fuktastic, both of whom remained silent and thoughtful, echoed Sax's sentiments.

Freakin' crazy mo-fos . . .

Yeah, crazy with a capital "K" . . .

Fuktastic gestured for silence and stepped up, a mere handsbreadth from Jade. His voice was one of cold, controlled fury. "Where do you get the *nuts* to waltz in 'ere with your new pussy little *billy no mates* boyfriend, askin' *us* to go to war *for him*?"

Jade felt a sense of sinking desperation, mixed with personal shame. Tastic had a point: She had used him, had led him on, leaving him wanting her. And now, here she had shown up hand in hand with Kar. Of course his feelings had been wounded. She shook her head, her expression humble. "It's not for him—it's for *all of us*."

Kar stepped up, squaring off with Tastic. "She's right, man. These bastards are the worst crew in history. We're not talkin' some Holocaust-denyin' skinheads from Ohio or New Jersey—we're talkin' one hard-core, old-school, *original* Nazi. We don't stop 'em tonight . . . the party's over . . . for all of us."

The crew exchanged looks of disbelief.

" 'Party's over,' my ass!" Sax exclaimed. "Who gives a shit what happens topside—once that storm blows over we'll still be down here, takin' care of bid'ness." He turned to Fuktastic. "Right, boss?"

Fuktastic didn't answer.

DV, whose dark, lovely face had remained somber and pensive up to this point, finally spoke. "You're forgettin' something, Sax." She gestured with her chin at Jade. "She's one of *us*. She asks us to go . . . we should be goin'."

Jade shot her a grateful look.

Sax waved a palm at Kar. "Wit' him?!"

Pee Wee nodded with certainty, raising himself to his full, diminutive height, his tone fearless. "Our girl's frontin' him, homes. Makes the boy righteous in my eyes—and far as them Nazis go? That shit is deep—like deep, deep in the *earth*. Goin' FMLN on their ass—that's like showin' mercy and proper love to all the rest of the world. So, yeah, I'm down—hell, I'm *double* down."

Big Buzz nodded. Giant though he was, he and little Pee Wee were tight; wherever Pee Wee went, Jade knew, Buzz was sure to follow.

"Make that triple," Buzz said.

Sax was wearing an *I-can't-believe-this-shit* expression. "Are you all *idiots*? This crew is supposed to be 'bout makin' *money*—what's in it for us?"

Kar glanced at Jade and shook his head. "I told her," he said under his breath.

Jade kept her expression solemn. Kar had, of course, told her nothing; he'd believed her when she said she'd be able to convince Tastic's crew to join them. But Kar was working the room, and Jade wasn't about to say anything to blow it for him.

Fuktastic fell for it. "Told her *what*?"

"Told her not to get her hopes up," Kar lied smoothly. "Told her this was tougher than boostin' ATM machines. Told her it was outta your league."

Diesel whipped out one of his blades and

jammed it up against Kar's throat. Jade tensed, but forced herself not to move.

Diesel gave one of his gap-toothed grins. "This punk's half right, you know? Nazis are some *tough mothers*—but see, thing is . . . we kick *their* ass, our rep goes Max with a capital 'M.' 'Sides . . ." He lowered the blade from Kar's throat and flipped it around in his hand. ". . . this is a *good chance* to cut some people."

Shade twirled his war clubs and nodded. "*And* put some hard wood to some soft balls."

Sax shook his head in utter frustration, then turned to Fuktastic. "Enough of this shit, y'all—this ain't no damn democracy. What do *you* say, boss?"

For a time, Fuktastic stood, contemplating it all in silence. Jade could feel the same tension she felt emanating from Kar; she had to remind herself to breathe during what seemed like an eternal silence. . . .

Then, at last, Fuktastic gave his verdict.

"Sometimes you do things for profit," he said carefully. "Other times 'cause it's the right thing to do." He paused. "You know . . . when I was born in the East End, within earshot of the church bells of Bow . . . my name was *Ira Greenblatt*. My mum's family . . . they got out of Europe just in time. But my dad's side . . . well, he was the only one who made it. My granddad . . ." He smiled fondly at the memory; it was, Jade thought, the tenderest expression she had ever seen on Tastic's face. "He was a tough ol' *four-by-two,* he was. Story is it took an *army* of stormtroopers to take out his proud Jewish ass." His tone turned reflective. "So what do I say . . . ?"

Suddenly, he jumped up onto his hydraulic lift and addressed the whole crew. *"I say: Are you ready to get* argee-bargee *on the goose-steppin' racist bastards who blitzed London and gave black leather a bad name?"*

Jade and Kar smiled at each other while the rest of the crew cheered.

12

In the dark, windowless room, the monk remained alone for a time, his eyes closed, his mind deep in meditation.

He could sense Kar's thoughts, and Jade's, see them as flashes of near-enlightenment just as clearly as he had seen the words of the scroll on Nina's computer screen, and he did his best to project his own thoughts to them. He knew he could trust his two young friends utterly to fulfill their joint destiny—or, at least, to die nobly trying.

Just as he was prepared to die in order to protect the world from the fury of the Four Elements. Colonel Struker believed he possessed everything because he now controlled the monk's body . . . but he would soon come to see that was not the case.

The monk opened his eyes at the sound of whirring overhead, then glanced up. The chains that bound his wrists and held him suspended hung from a mobile crane attached to the ceiling. The crane began to move along a track—dragging the hanging monk, swinging from his chains, out of the small, dark room and into a brightly lit room filled with consoles attended by white-coated men and women. Technicians of some sort, the monk decided, and then he caught sight of something that sent a thrill down his spine.

Against a long wall sat a gigantic contraption of gleaming metal—a modern torture device, with perhaps a dozen separate compartments the size of a human body. And in each compartment, his brother monks were fastened, their faces con-torted with pain, their skulls and *chi* points pierced with countless needles.

At the same time that the monk was grateful to see his brother monks alive, he also felt a momen-tary fear. For the device was Struker's design, pure Evil, designed for the most nefarious purposes.

But his enlightened will banished all terror at once. Now was not the time to yield to it—his mind had to be kept calm and clear if the world was to survive.

The ceiling crane dragged him past his brother monks, to an antechamber where the wizened Colonel Struker sat, his face half obscured by his oxygen mask, his withered arms and legs trem-bling, in a wheelchair.

At last, the crane carried the monk toward Struker, lowered him slightly, then stopped. The monk swung gently with the momentum and watched as the old man wheeled himself up close, less than an arm's distance away. Nearby, the flirtatious Nina and two of Struker's bodyguards watched intently.

Struker reached up, and with an unsteady, gnarled finger traced the Tibetan script tattooed on the monk's flesh.

"Look at me, monk," the colonel gasped. "For you, the years were nothing—you didn't change at all—but I withered and grew old."

Struker fell silent; his gaze grew distant, unfocused. He was, the monk knew, returning to an earlier time in his memory, a time sixty years past. And then his eyes cleared, and filled with a burning determination. Through sheer will—and nothing more—he rose up, wobbling, out of the wheelchair, then fell forward against the monk and wrapped feeble arms around him, holding on desperately.

He spoke, his breath fetid with approaching death. "Do you know," he said, his chin resting on the monk's shoulder, "that, after the war, everything that I loved . . . everything I believed in . . . was *destroyed*. And the little that was left . . . I had to betray in order to stay alive." He turned his head, his thin lips close to the monk's ear as he confided, "Can you imagine? The moment of your greatest victory . . . becomes the moment of your greatest *defeat*. Thanks to you . . ."

He leaned back and with every ounce of

strength—which was pathetically little—slapped the monk across the face with a cold palm.

The effort proved too much. Struker fell back, wheezing, into his chair.

The monk looked on him with the sincerest pity and compassion. Struker was truly the earthly incarnation of a hungry ghost—the epitome of self-hatred and grasping. His eyes glowed like coals with a thirst that could never be slaked. Even if Struker obtained the power of the scroll, he would never find a moment's peace, a moment's happiness.

When the colonel could at last speak again, his tone exuded a strange fondness. "And yet . . . the funny thing is . . . all that kept me from placing the muzzle of my Luger between my lips and blowing my brains to peaceful oblivion . . . was *you*." His gaze actually grew tender. "You—and the scroll." He paused. "You're my last chance to take everything that's gone wrong in this world since 1945 . . . *and make it right again*."

The old man started reading aloud the words of the Scroll of the Ultimate, his voice hoarse, rasping, tinged with a desperation beyond insanity. The words were ancient, eerie, yet at the same time, hauntingly beautiful. . . .

Yet read aloud in Struker's reedy, gasping voice, they were also capable of infinite evil. . . .

The monk closed his eyes.

In Fuktastic's hideout, Jade leaned over a table—her arm and shoulder pressed tightly against Kar, with whom she shared a fleeting smile—and studied the map that Tastic had un-rolled. It contained a grid of the crew's secret access and escape routes: all the underground tunnels, old subway lines, and sewer systems in the city.

Oddly, Jade felt the presence of the captured monk strongly, as if he were standing on her other side, in Tastic's place. She gazed at the schematic, at the juncture of two separate tunnels, each color-coded differently. She glanced quickly at the reference: one was a sewer tunnel, the other for water. It was as though the monk were speaking in her mind, saying: *Here. I am here.*

"Okay, we're *here*," Fuktastic said, echoing the words in Jade's head. He traced the map with a finger. "The sewer system and waterworks lead to *here* . . ." He glanced up in triumph. "Right below the Human Rights Building."

"I know the monk is down there," Kar said, with the same conviction Jade shared. "I can feel it. It's almost like he's talking to me."

She looked at him in amazement. "That's strange—I was just thinking the same thing."

Come quickly. The thought formed in Jade's head as if in reply—and the silent voice belonged to the monk. She turned to Tastic and his crew. "If we're gonna save him, we have to go *now*. Time's running out."

"Slow down!" Fuktastic ordered. "We can't go down there half-cocked." And in his best paramilitary style, he began barking commands at his crew. "We have to take 'em by surprise. Any guards, we clean 'em out as quickly and quietly as possible."

The crew understood: each member began prepping his or her weapons. Pee Wee seized his spray-paint cans, Sax some cigarette lighters, Diesel some butterfly knives, Shade some tire irons. As for DV, she started gathering up computer gear.

Through it all, Fuktastic kept talking. "Anybody from our crew goes down, we still stick to the plan—just don't leave 'em behind!"

Jade reached out and squeezed Kar's hand quickly—then let go even faster, slightly embarrassed to be seen showing such affection in front of Tastic and his crew. But she knew that, from this moment forward, she would never leave Kar behind.

Outside the Human Rights Organization Building, Struker's head bodyguard, Hermann Schmidt, held his automatic weapon at the ready, surrounded by his security team. Behind him was a stone fence, interrupted by a metal gate, and behind that, a stone tunnel leading to the courtyard and the building's front entry.

His men had already pledged their loyalty to him—and, ostensibly, to Nina Struker. *Foolish bitch*, Schmidt thought, smiling vaguely to himself. Nina was arrogant enough to think he could be won over by the promise of continued sexual favors, and stupid enough to think that Schmidt would never claim power for himself—and kill both her *and* the old man. Nina did not possess Struker's convictions, which Schmidt shared . . . and if she were untrustworthy enough to betray her own grandfather, Schmidt wanted nothing to do with her.

But supposedly, he and his loyal cadre now awaited Nina's signal to come and destroy the old man, once she was sure the power was attainable . . . and once she managed to distract the guards who still remained loyal to Struker.

The other reason Schmidt was waiting out in front of the HRO Building was because Struker had warned him that the American kid—the pickpocket—might be coming back to rescue the monk.

The old geezer had been serious—and it had been all Schmidt could do not to laugh aloud in his face. The kid might be good at getting away, but he was no match for Schmidt and his men.

Still, Schmidt leaned against the cold stone wall next to the metal gate, and stared out into the clear night. It would not be long, now, before all his years of silent obedience and seething at Struker's vicious abuse would be only a memory—and he would be free to take the power Struker so desperately sought. The old man had gone insane over the years, and Schmidt figured he was simply doing what was best for the Aryan race. The world should not be ruled by madmen: they were notoriously inefficient, and their megalomania eventually brought them down. Hitler had proven that.

As he gazed out into the night, headlights swept swiftly into view. One of his men gave a shout: the lights were headed this way—and instead of slowing down, the vehicle was speeding up!

That crazy kid, Schmidt thought, but he felt not the slightest anxiety. The bullets would take his car out before it ever hit the gate . . . and even if it *did* manage to get that far, the sturdy metal gate would crush the car like an aluminum can. Schmidt stepped away from the gate onto the sidewalk, as did his men, and raised his rifle.

As he did, a dark vehicle lurched toward them; Schmidt opened fire along with the rest of his team. The vehicle loomed closer now, screeching onto the sidewalk right at them, forcing the men to scatter onto the street—and it was then that Schmidt saw it clearly: a Suburban, with armor plating and black-tinted windows. The bullets bounced off it, harmless as pebbles.

He watched, jaw dropping, as the Suburban crashed through the heavy gate as if it were made of aluminum, not iron. The damned thing kept right on going, through the stone tunnel and into the courtyard beyond.

Inside Struker's headquarters, an alarm began to wail, drowning out the old man's reedy recitation of the sacred scroll.

To the monk, who still hung suspended from the ceiling in view of his brothers, Struker's chant had been blasphemous—and the sound of the alarm blessed. He knew precisely who had caused it, and to them he was deeply grateful. Hope blossomed in his heart like a lotus.

The former SS colonel, however, was stricken; he broke off reading, then twisted about in his chair to face Nina, his shriveled face even more puckered than usual with frustration. "Find out what's going on and put an end to it. *Now.*"

His tone carried a clear if implicit threat: If Nina was not able to stop the intruders, her own life would be forfeit. Nina seemed somewhat undone by the interruption—and the monk's Buddha-nature revealed to him that she had made her own plans to betray her grandfather.

The thought caused the monk sorrow: How pitiful, that grandfather and granddaughter could not trust each other, could not even experience so simple and wonderful a thing as familial love.

Yet the monk knew it was time to clear away such thoughts and instead focus on what was necessary: guiding the two good souls who were on their way not only to help a friend, but the entire world. He smiled slightly, and began to concentrate. . . .

The lead bodyguard, Schmidt, raced with the rest of his team into the courtyard. He was already shouting into his radio for backup—which proved to be unnecessary. The building's alarms and the noise of the Suburban crashing through the gate had caused other guards to come rushing outside.

Now the Suburban was racing for the building's front entry.

The guards near the entry emptied their weapons into the tires; there came the smell of burnt rubber as the tires dissolved into shreds. The vehicle skidded to a full stop.

Schmidt ran up behind the vehicle, then motioned for a couple of his men to back him up. Together, they cautiously neared, Schmidt's finger twitching on the trigger of his rifle.

And then an odd sight caught his eyes. The external lighting on the building glinted on the front windshield, allowing Schmidt for an instant to see inside.

There didn't seem to be anyone there.

Impossible, Schmidt thought. But at the very least, no one had come out of the vehicle or fired from it. He signaled once again for his men to move close beside him, the barrels of their weapons pointed at the driver's seat of the Surburban, then he leaned forward and cupped a hand around his eyes in order to see through the window.

He'd been right: there was no one in there—just a device rigged to the steering wheel and gas pedal. And his eyes went wide—very wide—at the sight of the detonator sitting where the human driver should be.

Schmidt reared back and opened his mouth to shout a warning to his team: too late. In one instant, the dark Suburban was standing there; and in the next, it dissolved into a hail of twisted metal shrapnel and flames.

Abruptly blinded, Schmidt felt his body being lifted up and hurled back—back against something hard and unyielding, something that caused a sharp, stabbing pain in his back and head, something that ultimately dissolved into nothingness, darkness. . . .

In an underground tunnel beneath the Human Rights Organization, DV shut her laptop with an authoritative "mission accomplished" air, then turned to Fuktastic and gave him the thumbs-up.

"Ka-*boom*," she said.

Down in the building's subbasement, Nina— accompanied by two bodyguards—froze at the sudden explosion overhead. The floor beneath her feet shuddered slightly; the lights flickered on and off, causing her to hold her breath and wait for another blast.

It never came. The lights at last steadied; Nina released a sigh, then resumed her relentless search for the intruders—who, according to the security scanners, were *not* at the explosion site.

But she knew Schmidt was—and that filled her with a simmering rage. Had Struker discovered her plan to topple him? Was this search a ploy, an attempt to send her to her death?

Or was this, in fact, what it appeared to be—the monk's foolish young friend, thinking he could actually rescue him?

Either way, Nina vowed silently, whoever had just foiled her plan would be made to pay.

Deep in the silent, catacomb-like tunnels that ran beneath the city streets, Kar was feeling more energized, more alive, than he ever had in his life. He was finally precisely where he belonged, doing precisely what he was meant to be doing. Best of all, Jade was by his side.

They were making their way through a dark, claustrophobically low-ceilinged tunnel alongside Fuktastic and the crew. Sax led the way, squinting at the map using a penlight.

When they'd all heard the explosion overhead, Kar could feel the exhilaration that rippled through the crowd. Even now, Fuktastic was still smiling.

"Nice plan, Kar," he said. "Misdirection and speed."

Kar grinned at him, unable to resist a little jab at his former nemesis. "Thanks, *Ira.*"

Fuktastic's expression soured as he shot Kar a feigned Look of Death.

Sax stopped abruptly and raised an arm to point

overhead. Kar and the rest of the gang followed his gaze upward, to a heavy steel grating.

"Right here is the old water main that should put us inside," Sax announced.

Kar stepped up and pressed with all his strength against it—

Remember, you can do anything, you can walk on air, you can swim in it, you can travel to the highest peaks in the Himalayas if you only believe. . . .

But what do you do about cold steel?

Kar pushed until his muscles gave way completely. Exhausted, gasping, he fell back and examined the grating more closely.

A heavy industrial bolt held it firmly in place.

Buzz—big, hulking, muscle-bound Buzz—shoved past Kar with the indulgent grin of a parent watching a toddler trying to tackle an adult task. "Step aside, finger-man. Let a big white boy do his thing."

Kar wasn't about to argue. He watched, impressed, as Buzz grabbed hold of the grating with both hands; the muscles in the large man's arms and shoulders bulged impressively, and his broad face grew red with strain. But at last the grating came free, and Buzz dropped it to the concrete floor with a loud clang, then grinned at the crew.

"After you," he said.

Kar shot him a look both affectionate and teasing. "Show-off."

One by one, they crawled up into the water main and raced off into the darkness.

They had gone less than a quarter-mile when they encountered a fork in the tunnel system. Sax stopped, mystified, poring over his map; Fuktastic turned to Kar, in recognition of who was *really* in charge.

"Do we hit 'em with a right," Fuktastic asked, "or a left?"

Kar looked at Fuktastic—yet somehow, he had the sense he was seeing *beyond* him as well, to the place where the monk was trapped. At the same time, he fancied he could hear the monk's voice echoing softly from the right-hand fork.

He pointed to it. "This way!"

He broke into a stealthy half run, the others following close behind.

Several hundred yards beyond, they rounded a corner—and came face-to-face with a massive iron door. Sax checked his map.

"This is it."

Kar looked at the door, discouraged, while Fuktastic inspected the door, then put into words what Kar was thinking.

"Two tons of steel and hydraulic locks." Fuktastic turned to Buzz. "No way you're gonna rip this baby off the wall, mate."

"Relax." DV stepped forward, as always calm and collected, and pulled a palm-sized LED device from her pocket—the same thing, Kar remembered, from a night that seemed a thousand years distant, that she had used to break the code on the ATM back at Fuktastic's hideout. "I'm on it," she said.

And in a display of technical brilliance every bit as impressive as Buzz's muscularity, she plugged the device into the door's computer locking system and began punching buttons.

Kar was no computer scientist, but he *was* smart enough to figure out what she was doing, and grinned at the realization: She was reprogramming the lock.

With utter confidence, DV finished her work, then began to count. "In three—two—one . . ."

The click that followed was soft, but to Kar's ears it was louder and more triumphant than the explosion had been; the massive door swung open slightly, and he made his way through, holding it open so that Jade and the others could follow.

Kar wheeled around the next bend—and immediately found himself less than a hundred yards from two of Struker's heavily armed Suits. One of them grinned at him and raised his weapon.

Kar froze.

Beside him, Fuktastic pulled a rattling canister from his pockets with a lightning reflex that impressed even a skilled pickpocket like Kar. With his peripheral vision, Kar watched as Fuktastic hurled what looked like an aerosol can, with a flash of silver and blue, at the Suits.

It exploded into aluminum shrapnel, flames . . .

and brilliant blue paint. A spray-paint-can bomb, Kar realized. The ear-shattering blast felled the Suits at once; Kar and the others hurried past their paint-spattered bodies.

Behind Fuktastic, Jade piped up, her tone one of clear annoyance. "Quick *and* quiet, remember?"

She had a point—but Tastic chose to be irritated. "How 'bout a thank-you?"

Jade rolled her eyes—but Kar just kept on moving, forcing the others to keep a swift pace. He felt as though the monk was whispering in his ears.

Time grows short. The danger of the Four Elements unbound is very near. . . .

Ahead of all the others, he ran around another corner . . .

. . . and once again, found his way blocked—this time by a larger group of menacing Suits. One of them smiled evilly and aimed his weapon at Kar's skull.

Kar immediately skidded to a stop and ducked back around the corner; he motioned for Fuktastic's crew to wait. "How 'bout an 'Oh, shit'?"

The monk's voice again, in his head: *Help lies nearby.*

Kar surveyed his surroundings. There was nothing—nothing but dark concrete walls, darkness, the uncertain crew . . . and a circular iron wheel on the tunnel wall. Inspiration dawned, as a detail from Sax's map of underground burrows surfaced in Kar's memory.

He grabbed the cold handle and tried to turn it; it wouldn't budge.

Sax immediately shoved himself between Kar and the wheel. "Fool! You wanna get us all drowned?"

Filled with righteous certainty, Kar stood his ground, and when he spoke, it was in a tone that allowed for no argument—there was no time for such things. "According to your map, this is a manual flush for the storm tank. It'll release the rain from earlier tonight on *them* and the water should keep going till it hits the treatment station—*below us.*"

Sax looked to his leader—Fuktastic. Kar held his breath.

Tastic's eyes were dark, unreadable . . . and then he waved Sax aside with a short, sharp motion.

Kar stepped up and, gritting his teeth, grasped the wheel lock and turned with every ounce of his physical strength. At first, the wheel refused again to move.

If I could reach Jade's window—fly through the air—then I sure as hell can do this.

The wheel shuddered, then let go a great, screeching groan as it finally turned.

Kar heard the low rumble even before the water came . . . just as the Suits were rounding the bend.

It cascaded down in front of Kar and the crew with a deafening roar, splashing full force down onto the tunnel floor. It surged toward the approaching Suits like a raging river, so swiftly that they had no time to turn and flee, but were knocked from their feet.

Kar watched as the flood carried them back the way they had come.

Fuktastic regarded Kar with astonished approval. "Maybe you *are* Fuktastic material."

13

Inside his control room, Struker continued his rasping chant of the Tibetan words on the computer screen, magnified so that even he could make them out with his failing eyesight. The task was difficult; even though he had increased the flow of oxygen to his mask to make the recitation easier, his lungs were burning, and he felt he could not catch his breath. His greatest fear was that he would faint from the strain before he was able to finish—in which case, Nina or one of his own men would most certainly take advantage of his weakness and kill him.

It was the way of Nature: the strong preyed on the weak. This had always made sense to Struker and he had always abided by this principle, and in theory still clung to it . . . though he greatly despised the fact that he was no longer one of the strong.

But he intended to become one again—if only he could hold on long enough to finish the ancient chant. Right now, he was more spent than he had ever been as a young man leading the arduous trek through the Himalayas.

The old man felt a sudden chill. Exhaustion and excitement, he thought, but then he saw the breeze ruffling the hair of the technicians and bodyguards, and watched as papers began to rustle on counters, then were lifted up into the air. . . .

The breeze turned into a strong, gusting wind that swept the chamber, filling it with a strange hum.

Struker began to convulse. *I'm dying,* he thought, with bitter frustration. *So close, and now I'm dying. . . .*

The convulsions gave way to the most intense pain Struker had ever experienced. He was an SS commander; he knew how to push himself beyond his physical limits, beyond pain. He'd had a bullet removed in the battlefield without anesthetic, and he had not cried out then.

But he screamed now, in the purest agony. It began in his chest, then radiated out until every single inch of his withered body was affected.

Yet in the midst of his pain, Struker came to himself, opened his eyes, forced himself to continue his recitation of the scroll.

And the pain transformed itself into something Struker almost did not recognize at first: strength.

Still chanting, he rose easily, lightly from his

wheelchair, dazzled by the sudden radiance that emanated from the monk's body and entered Struker's own.

The sensation was pure euphoria: Struker felt his rib cage enlarge, his spine straighten, his lungs expand. . . . He watched, overjoyed, as the shrunken, flabby flesh on his arm grew firm and rippled with muscle. He put a hand to his head, felt the thick head of newly grown hair, and smiled.

He stepped away from his wheelchair, up to the gleaming mechanical device that housed the captured monks, and admired his own reflection. He was young and strong again, a man of thirty, just as he was when he had first encountered the monk.

Even the scar left by that damned monkey was missing.

Struker grinned up at the monk, still suspended from the ceiling . . . and, as he had sixty years ago, before murdering the monks high in the Tibetan Himalayas, did a few steps of a Tibetan folk dance.

With Jade beside him, Kar continued on through the underground labyrinth, followed by Fuktastic and his group.

Abruptly, Kar stopped, seized by a sudden wordless conviction, and knelt down to touch a rusty grating on the wet concrete floor. "Here. He's down *here.*"

Jade nodded, her wide gaze meeting Kar's.

Whatever messages Kar was hearing from the monk, it was clear she heard them, too. "He's right."

Lean and wiry Pee Wee dropped to the floor and put his ear to the grating—from the reactions of the crew members, Kar assumed that Pee Wee had the best hearing of them all. Everyone was silent for a long moment.

Pee Wee confirmed Kar's intuition with a nod. "You can hear a generator."

At once, he recoiled in fear and disgust—leaping backward and almost knocking Kar off his feet—as two large black rats scurried out from the grating. From his Medusa-faced expression, Kar assumed Pee Wee and rats didn't get along all that well.

Fuktastic grinned. "Desertin' their sinking ship."

"I hate rats!" Pee Wee shuddered.

"I love 'em," Buzz said, in a surprisingly tender tone for such a tough-looking hulk of muscle. "I had a pet rat when I was a kid."

Making sure he could be heard by both Buzz *and* Pee Wee, Diesel turned to Sax with a chip-toothed grin. "I love to *eat* rats."

DV shook her head at them like an annoyed den mother. "Yo—rat boyz! Let's go!"

Sax rolled his eyes at the lot while Kar and Jade busied themselves with the grate. Between the two of them, it came up easily.

Kar dropped first into the pipe; Jade followed. It was slow going: the entire pipe was covered with green slime, making for treacherous footing. The place was filled with different sounds: the hum of a generator, the rushing of water through other tunnels, a constant drip overhead . . . and, of course, the constant scurrying of rats.

Above them, Fuktastic, Sax, Diesel, and the others were lowering themselves down through the narrow grating as well; Pee Wee was next-to-last, then Buzz. As always, Pee Wee stuck close to Buzz. He felt an undying loyalty to the big square brick: It was Buzz who had saved Pee Wee's ass one day, when he was being beaten almost to death by a different gang, back when he was working alone. Seven guys, all kicking the hell out of Pee Wee, who'd never stood a chance and was already saying his Ave Marias, waiting to die.

Then Buzz had arrived on the scene. Pee Wee had expected the nasty-looking big white dude to be the death knell: Here his own *cholos* were knocking the shit out of him—why should he expect this white guy to do anything more than help finish him off?

But Buzz had taken offense—*major* offense. When he had opened that ugly, broad face of his to say, "How 'bout let's make this a little more even, amigos?," Pee Wee knew he would never be able to repay the guy, ever.

Now, the rest of Fuktastic's crew had lowered themselves down into the pipe: only Pee Wee and

Buzz were left. Pee Wee leaped down nimbly—no problem.

Then all at once, the crew heard the sound of rapid footsteps—a whole lot of particularly wicked-sounding footsteps—closing in.

"*Shit!*" Fuktastic swore. "Move it, people!"

Pee Wee gestured to his friend, suddenly worried. He looked at the size of the narrow grate opening, and the size of Buzz, and saw nothing but trouble coming. "Buzz, *come on!*"

Buzz placed a leg into the opening, then another leg, using his burly arms to lower himself down—but got no farther than midthigh.

The opening was simply not big enough to let him pass.

The footsteps were closer—another few seconds, Pee Wee realized with horror, and the Nazi's men would be breathing down their necks.

"Go," Buzz said calmly. He popped himself back out of the opening and picked up the grating as if it weighed no more than a feather. "I'll buy you some time."

Pee Wee tried to count the footsteps. There had to be at least six men headed for them. "*No!*" he shrieked. "*Buzz!*"

In reply, Buzz slammed the grating down on them.

Overhead came the sound of footsteps arriving—followed by Buzz's shouts, the sounds of flesh colliding with flesh, bone with bone, then gunfire . . .

Then silence.

Pee Wee leaped for the grating, caught hold of it, and tried to yank it aside.

Firmly, but gently, Fuktastic pulled him down, and motioned for him to remain quiet.

Pee Wee could only obey. He had to do what the boss said, and what was best for the crew—but he still couldn't help feeling he had failed his one truest friend.

He turned to the rest of the group, helpless and hating himself, and saw grim expressions on every face.

"C'mon," Fuktastic said grimly.

And so they went, against the background noise of water roaring through pipes.

Struker thrust young, muscular arms to the sky in a gesture of pure triumph as golden, glittering power emanated from his body. He felt euphoric to the point of mania, and beyond: the world was his now, after all these years, and he would achieve the dream the Führer had failed to.

With vision now so keen he felt he could see every mote of dust, every atom shimmering in the air, Struker read the Tibetan script from the computer screen in a voice so youthful, so strong and masculine he fought to keep from breaking into joyous laughter.

These were the words of the Scroll of the Ultimate; the words that would give him power over the Four Elements, the power to reshape the entire world.

"Om ah hum vajra guru padma . . ." he chanted, then abruptly stopped.

Complete power was not his; this he sensed, as well as the fact that linguistically, the syntax made no sense. The chant had broken off abruptly.

The scroll was not complete.

For a moment, Struker stared at the computer screen in disbelief; then he whirled on the monk and asked in English, in a voice that sounded petulant and weak to his own ears, "Where . . . *where's the rest of it?"*

The monk hung from his chains in silence.

Struker reared back with his right arm, then delivered a brutal blow to the monk's midsection, and felt somewhat mollified by the sounds of ribs cracking. This time, his tone turned harsh. *"WHERE'S THE LAST VERSE?"*

The monk coughed up a bit of blood, then gave Struker one of his annoyingly enlightened smiles. "I memorized it—just in case someone like you managed to get this far."

Struker's eyes widened with disbelief and fury; he let go a howl of pure rage and, with inhuman strength, tore the monk from the chains that bound him to the ceiling crane.

The monk landed softly on his feet. Years ago, Struker would have been terrified of the monk's power—but now he grasped the monk's arms firmly and forced him over to the vast machine where his fellow Tibetan monks were imprisoned.

"Fine," Struker snarled. *"I'll suck it out of your brain instead!"*

The monk struggled, but he was no match for Struker's newfound might. The German smashed the monk's head into the machine and brutally jammed electronic needles and probes into the monk's skull.

Stimulated by the electrical activity of the Tibetan's brain, the machine hummed to life.

Struker grinned as holographic imagery began to form in the very air in front of the monk. Even so, the Brother With No Name fought to resist with all his power: Struker's smile broadened as perspiration began to drip from the monk's brow, as tears streamed from his eyes.

But the images were not yet readable. With sadistic pleasure, Struker brought the machine up to full, killing power.

The monk screamed in agony . . . and Tibetan symbols shimmered, gossamer, in the air in front of him.

The last verse of the Scroll of the Ultimate.

"Yes!" Struker shouted, exultant. "Yessss . . ."

Smiling, he began once more to read aloud.

Inside the water main, Kar was moving as fast as possible without his feet slipping out from beneath him on the moldy surface. "Keep going!" he urged Jade and the others. "We're almost there. . . ."

But for all his bravado, he had sensed something dreadful: the monk's pain. He could no longer hear the monk's calm voice, and knew that the unthinkable was on the verge of happening: Struker was very, very close to seizing ultimate power.

Kar glanced up at the sound of rushing water in front of him—growing ever nearer.

"Shit!" Sax said behind him. "Did you close that manual flush after you opened it?"

Uh-oh, Kar was about to say, but he never got a chance to voice the words. A wall of water was coming, roaring straight at them.

Fuktastic and his crew ducked into a right-hand fork in the tunnel and began pulling each other up to safety. It only seemed right to Kar, since he was the idiot who left the flush open, to be last in line.

And that proved his undoing.

As Jade reached her hand down for him, he was hit by the water. Kar tried to hang on . . . but the current was too strong. It hurtled him through the pipe like a cannonball.

Somehow, he managed to raise his head long enough to fill his lungs with air; somehow he managed to keep his mouth closed and not swallow water.

Somehow, he managed to keep his wits about himself long enough to question *why*—if the monk's story was true, and everything so far had proven the monk to be right, and he and Jade had both seemed to be reading the monk's mind—was he, Kar, going to drown in a crummy, slimy water pipe beneath the city? Somehow, it didn't seem like an event the monk would deem "appropriate karma."

Kar's wet ride didn't last long—just long enough for him to consider the question, and then he was thrown out of the pipe, against a sluice, and onto a floor. He sucked in air with a gasp, but the sound was masked by the gurgle of the water draining.

Dazed, he was able to lift his head just high enough to realize that he was someplace wickedly strange . . . in a vast room that housed a kinky-looking metal device the size of several SUVs parked end-to-end. . . .

And in that device, the monks from the secret temple beneath the pottery factory were strapped in tight.

Kar lifted his head a little higher—and saw a young, blond German man, his body glowing with power. . . .

And his heart sank at once.

He knew he looked upon Colonel Struker—a ninety-year-old man, the same crazed Nazi who had been trying to capture the monk all these years. Only this was Struker transformed, which meant he had gained the power of the Ultimate. But something was missing. . . . Struker did not yet have power over the Four Elements, so he had not yet finished his recitation of the scroll.

Kar lifted his chin a bit more, and felt pain in his heart at the sight of the monk, stripped and beaten, his head pierced by a dozen probes. . . .

And, shimmering in the air between the monk and the Nazi, hovered the words that could save or destroy the universe. . . .

In the corridor, Jade led the way swiftly, trying to maintain her confidence, but although she still sensed the monk's presence, she also sensed great desperation emanating from him. Worse, she deathly worried that Kar had drowned. . . .

But she kept reassuring herself that she would somehow have sensed that.

Mystical bullshit. It's all unraveling, girl. Can't you see you just wanted *to believe it was all true?*

It is *all true, and you* know *it, Jade. It may be mystical, but it's not bullshit. You've been waiting all your life for this to happen. You just never admitted it to yourself before.*

The group moved along behind her in grim silence, until Sax at last spoke up, echoing Jade's own thoughts.

"This is bullshit, man!" He came to a dead stop. "We should turn around and get the hell out of here, *now.*"

Jade wheeled on him. "We have to find Kar and the monk!"

Sax's bottom lip curled. "Speak for yourself, sweet meat." He turned and took off in the opposite direction.

Pee Wee, Diesel, and DV all watched him go . . . and then they turned to face Fuktastic, awaiting orders.

Jade turned to him as well. "Please." There was no feigned seductiveness in her tone; she honestly regretted that she had ever led him on, ever misused him, and she hoped he understood that. But she needed her friends now—all the friends she could get—and she looked on Tastic as one.

Fuktastic took a long, deep breath, then at last replied, "We started something—*let's finish it.*"

Jade began to smile at him—but her smile faded before it ever bloomed.

The wind howled eerily through the tunnel, causing the skin on the back of Jade's neck to prickle, and her hair to lash against her face; she sensed the presence of true evil. The power surged with an electrical hum; overhead, the lights began to strobe on and off, making her surroundings surreal.

"DON'T MOVE!" a harsh, feminine voice ordered—a voice Jade recognized immediately, for it had given her a chill once more. This time, the hatred and sadism in it was completely unmasked and raw—but Jade still knew it belonged to the executive director of the Human Rights Organization.

In the pulsating light, the director approached, coldly seductive in a tight-fitting tailored suit and stiletto pumps, her blond hair pulled back tightly from her elaborately made-up face. Darkness again, then another flash of light, and Jade could see the vicious rage in the blond woman's eyes, in her taut expression. In one delicate hand, the long nails painted the color of blood, the director held an automatic pistol aimed directly at Jade's skull.

Accompanying the blond woman was a squad of armed bodyguards. The strobing light gave them a ghostly, otherworldly appearance—*hungry ghosts,* Jade thought, remembering what her old Tibetan language instructor had once taught her—that might well have seemed terrifying to most.

But Jade put all fear aside. An odd conviction seized her: that she had been born for this moment, had trained her entire life for it. This confrontation was her destiny, and regardless of the outcome, she was ready to embrace it.

She called out to Tastic and his team. *"LET'S DO IT!"*

A close quarters, all-out battle erupted in the tunnel, as Jade and Fuktastic's crew rushed the blonde and her Nazi bodyguards.

A sudden surge of power flowed through Jade's body, one both mental and physical: she felt as though she had been hooked into a mystical Source which conferred preternaturally keen awareness of all that happened around her and to her.

Several things were occurring simultaneously.

Pee Wee, fueled by grief and rage over the loss of his closest friend, leaped onto the tallest guard and wrapped his small arms around the Nazi's neck. The big man fought to pull the smaller off, but Pee Wee was tenacious; he tightened his grip with one arm, then freed one hand and started pummeling the guard's face and skull, all the while shouting. *"Mató a Buzz, pendejo! YOU KILLED BUZZ!"*

DV was putting her physical agility to good use. As two guards approached her, guns drawn, she zigzagged between them, cleverly avoiding their aim until she tricked them into opening fire—and inadvertently shooting each other.

In the meantime, Fuktastic pulled out another can of spray paint and blasted it into the eyes of a few guards, blinding them—at which point he brought them all down easily with a few martial-arts blows Jade had taught him.

Shade wielded his war clubs with impressive skill, distracting a pair of guards from firing at him until he was at last able to deal a couple of whirling blows that knocked the two men senseless.

As for Jade, she watched as if in slow motion as one of the guards raised his weapon and pointed it directly at her, then tensed his finger on the trigger . . .

. . . at which point Diesel hurled a knife, which slashed through the air like a streak of silver lightning, and impaled the back of the gun-wielder's hand. The guard screamed, his fingers spasming straight outward; the pistol fell from his grip. Bullets sprayed forth, going wide and ripping through an overhead pipe.

Water sprayed down on the group in a cold torrent.

During the fight, the blond woman had somehow lost her weapon—but now she took advantage of the distraction to launch a deadly blow at Jade.

Jade eluded the blow, instead curling herself into a ball and flipping through the air, over the director's head—landing behind the woman. Jade aimed a swift, short chop at the blonde's neck and sent her down hard onto the wet concrete. The woman's hair, darkened by the rain, now hung in limp, bedraggled locks against her narrow face.

But the blonde was not so easily dispensed with. She instantly pushed herself up from the ground, spun about, and threw her entire body against Jade's side. Jade went down, her forehead and nose smashing against the wet, hard ground; her long hair spread out around her, soaking up the standing water.

Standing over her, the director laughed and triumphantly raised one fist into the air—then began to bring it down with killer force toward Jade's skull.

Jade immediately rolled to her side and reached for the iron sewer grate beside her. It was incredibly solid and heavy—it should, in fact, have been nearly impossible for her to lift, yet because her mind had no time to register that fact, her muscles responded with inhuman speed.

She yanked the grate up and out and held it between herself and the blonde—blocking the blow slicing through the air toward her.

Jade heard the dull crunch as the director's knuckles broke against the solid metal. The blonde staggered backward, howling with agony as she clutched the wrist of her wounded hand.

Jade rolled to her feet. By the time she faced the other woman again, the blonde had recovered enough to reach into a shoulder holster hidden beneath her soaked suit jacket, and pulled out two devices that looked like cordless microphones . . . with blue-gold electrical sparks spitting from the ends.

Stun batons, Jade realized . . . and here they were, completely surrounded by water.

She tensed, preparing for her next strike.

14

Hidden behind Struker's infernal machine, Kar watched as the monk writhed, struggling against the restraints that held him fast. Swirling, glittering energy emanated from the cruel probes stuck into the monk's scalp, then moved down the cords and into the computer, which generated holographic Tibetan script that filled the air. And as Struker continued to chant each word as it formed, more energy surged from his new, youthful body.

Just as Jade had, Kar felt no fear; instead he felt a surge of righteous power and conviction as to what he *had* to do.

He leaped for the chain hanging from the ceiling crane. He should not have been able to reach it—but he did, easily, because he did not allow himself to consider failure. He swung up and through the air, over the gleaming machine where the monk and the brothers of the secret temple suffered, through the swirls of pure energy and the spiraling holographs of Tibetan script.

"LET HIM GO!" Kar demanded, and was amazed at the depth of authority and strength in his own voice.

He jumped down from the chain just in front of the now awesomely powerful and young Struker; before the surprised Nazi could react, Kar struck out with a barrage of kung-fu blows.

While the bodyguards continued to move in on Fuktastic's crew, Jade and the blonde were still circling each other—the latter clutching a stun baton in each hand, despite the rapid swelling of her now-purple knuckles. *She's holding onto it through sheer will*, Jade knew—but she also knew her own will was even stronger.

They lunged at each other, eluded each other, then went back to circling again.

The blonde sneered at Jade. "You can't win. My grandfather was the number-one hand-to-hand combat master in Hitler's SS and he taught me everything he knows!"

So, Jade realized. This was Struker's own granddaughter. Maybe there *was* something to karma—certainly, this evil had been passed down through generations. "Oh, yeah?" she countered. "Well, my dad's the top man in the *Russian mafia* and he taught me everything *he* knows!"

She moved in swiftly, lashing out with arms and

a leg—and immediately recoiled as Struker the younger applied the stun batons. It was like being stung by a thousand hornets, but Jade forced herself to recover, and regain her balance.

The blonde took advantage of Jade's instant of disorientation to charge, swinging wildly with the batons, scraping floor and ceiling. In the pulsating light and darkness, blue sparks flew; Jade avoided them, knowing that any exposure to water would make the electrical charge far more intense.

That thought led her to inspiration: From a standing position, she executed a three-hundred-sixty-degree flip, ending up with her heels pushing hard into the blond Nazi's solar plexus.

Struker's granddaughter went flying backward into the tunnel . . .

. . . and wound up lying on her back in a pool of water, manicured hands still clutching the stun batons. She spasmed in agony, her entire body haloed by a hundred small blue lightning bolts as the voltage coursed through her. At last her head lolled as she faded into unconsciousness; even still, her body convulsed, enveloped in the miniature electrical storm.

Jade spoke, knowing that she would not be heard. "Blackout, baby."

But her sense of victory soon faded; she glanced up to see that the bodyguards had almost succeeded in cornering Fuktastic and his crew, and were moving in with their pistols raised. She prepared to launch herself at the guards. She'd be directly in the line of fire, but her own death no longer mattered to her: what was important was saving her friends, so they in turn could survive to save Kar and the monk.

Without them, she realized with a sudden tug at her heart, her own life would have no meaning.

She tensed her muscles and crouched, readying herself . . .

. . . when, farther down the tunnel, beyond the looming guards, a metal door smashed open, ringing loudly as a clanging church bell against the concrete wall. Before the startled guards could react, a huge, hulking figure threw himself at them like a deranged linebacker, and knocked them to the ground; their pistols skidded across the wet floor, and Fuktastic and his crew hurried to pick them up.

The hulking figure looked up . . . and in the strobing light, Jade smiled hugely.

Buzz himself was bruised and bloody, his clothing torn, but the grin on his face could have been no wider. "The white boy," he announced, to his overjoyed crew members, "has done his thang."

Inside Struker's lair, the monk watched as Kar and Struker did battle.

"You little *race traitor!*" Struker shouted.

In reply, Kar unleashed a flying kick that struck the Nazi full in the face, with devastating force. Struker fell to his knees.

"You're the one who's a traitor to your race, man—the *human* race!"

The monk felt a fresh stab of pain in his skull . . . he grimaced, squeezing his eyes tightly shut; when he opened them again, he saw that another phrase in Tibetan script had materialized in the air in front of Struker.

The German read it aloud . . . and his young, muscular body began to emanate even more glittering energy. He raised a hand and pointed it at Kar: the American was lifted from his feet and hurled against a wall.

Kar struck the wall, slid to the floor, and lay there, dazed.

At the sight, the monk forced himself to master all doubt, to believe in the impossible. True, Struker was now too powerful for the monk to contain; indeed, he had just acquired the magical power of levitation, an ability known only to the greatest mystical adepts. True, the monk had been greatly weakened by the loss of mental and physical energy the machine had drained from him. True, everything should be lost, and the monk should just yield. . . .

Om ah hung vajra guru padma siddhi hung . . .

Oh, Vajra Guru, beloved Padmasambhava, grant us the magical powers and abilities we need to attain enlightenment . . .

Grant us the impossible.

The monk broke through his restraints, freeing arms and legs in a burst of sudden strength. With a single movement of his hand, the monk gathered together the separate probes piercing his skull and pulled them free.

Then he threw himself at Struker, who was still gloating over the fallen Kar.

The German spun about, evading the monk and answering with a vicious blow. The monk blocked the blow, then struck out with his right arm, sending Struker crashing to the floor.

In response, the prone Struker used his legs and feet to sweep the monk off balance; the monk fell atop the German, and instantly locked arms with his nemesis.

For a few seconds, the monk and Struker were face-to-face, eye-to-eye; Struker's breath was warm against the monk's skin. The German's strength seemed invincible; the monk struggled not to give way against it, but the muscles in his arms, hands, and shoulders began to quiver slightly with the effort.

Oh, Vajra Guru, beloved Padmasambhava . . .

The monk silently chanted to himself, knowing it was not the specific words that made the prayer so powerful, but the intent in his own heart. More than anything, he wished for Struker's enlightenment, for all that was sincerely good to come to Struker, that Struker might be freed from his obsession with evil and instead know true bliss. . . .

The trembling in the monk's limbs ceased; calmness overtook him, and any trace of unenlightened human resentment or anger he might have felt toward Struker on account of the harm the Nazi had done his brother monks and Kar immediately left him. Instead, his heart was filled with goodwill.

Strength filled him; he found he could increase his grip on Struker's hands, even begin to force the German's arms back toward the floor.

There came a crack as Struker's index finger snapped from the strain. The German roared aloud with pain and fury; at once, he bent his knees, then lifted the monk's torso onto the soles of his feet. From there, he quickly let go with his hands and launched the monk with a fierce kick against the wall.

The monk hit it with such force the breath was knocked from him; around him, plaster shattered and went flying.

By the time the monk regained his feet, Struker charged him, lashing out with a fresh blow—one the monk easily dodged. He grasped Struker's arm and, in a gesture much like cracking a whip, sent the Nazi whirling end over end across the room.

Now Struker hit the wall, sending even more plaster flying.

Even from a distance, the monk could see rage flaring in Struker's pale eyes; the German let go a howl of rage, then once again resorted to the magical powers conferred on him by his incomplete recitation of the scroll. He lifted an arm and motioned at Brother Tenzin.

At once, the leader of the secret temple was torn from his restraints, and his helpless body was launched, a projectile, at the monk.

The monk had no choice: he sailed through the air and caught poor Brother Tenzin the instant before he was smashed against the wall.

The distraction afforded Struker the opportunity to wreak more havoc. With another gesture, he sent heavy metal bolts popping out of the walls and directed them, deadly missiles, at the monk.

The monk laid Tenzin gently aside and still managed to avoid each one—but Struker was merely starting his attack. Now he attacked the monk full-force, throwing punches so powerful that with each blow, crackles of pure energy emanated from his body.

"Give up and join your brothers," Struker demanded through gritted teeth, "the ones I left dead in the mountains of Tibet half a century ago! Give up and you can finally have peace! *Why make this so hard on yourself?*"

The monk gazed on Struker with a defiance born of wisdom, not anger. "Hard is birth," he proclaimed. "Hard is life . . . Hard is the appearance of a buddha . . ."

As he spoke, a recovered Kar made his way over to the two struggling men, and launched an attack at Struker, trying to get him to free the monk.

But the German had become too strong; Kar's attack clearly annoyed him, but it was not enough to allow the monk to pull out of Struker's grasp.

Om ah hung vajra guru . . .

Yet Kar had barely begun to help when Jade appeared, accompanied by the group the monk recognized as Mista Fuktastic and his gang.

Jade's clothes and hair were soaked, as were the others', and her face was bruised and dirtied—but she struck out at the former SS colonel with such concentration and strength that the monk was truly amazed. She landed two blows on Struker's arms—the second one a direct hit on the German's broken finger, which caused him to groan and release his grip on the monk—then followed with a kick that knocked him back a few steps.

Now, the monk realized with deep gratefulness to his friends and to the Vajra Guru, it was three against one, with himself, Jade, and Kar teaming up against Struker; now the monk knew himself to be invincible. Now he could truly *believe*.

The trio immediately encircled the German.

The monk locked gazes with Struker and smiled. ". . . And hard is the *beating* one must occasionally deliver to those who know not the Sublime Truth."

Fear flickered in the Nazi's eyes. He made a last, desperate charge at the monk . . .

. . . who embraced him and flipped him up onto the ceiling crane. The hook caught hold of Struker's shirt, and the monk grabbed hold of the hanging man and sent him hurtling across the control room.

Such was Struker's momentum that, when the

crane could go no farther, he went flying off the hook and crashing into his computers.

Sparks shot out from the controls; the lights flickered as his monstrous device began to lose power and shut down.

As for Struker, he slumped to the floor, unconscious.

The monk felt no joy at his enemy's defeat, only sorrow that the man had chosen to turn to evil. But he was glad to join with the others—Kar, Jade, and Mista Fuktastic's group—in setting his brother monks free from their restraints, and he was relieved that the world had been rescued from oblivion.

Once the others were freed, the monk hurried over to Tenzin, who still huddled on the floor.

"Brother Tenzin—?" he asked, with gentle concern.

Tenzin looked up at him, his dark eyes filled with humility and regret. A wordless moment passed between them, one in which the monk understood what had happened with Tenzin's protégé, and how much the leader of the secret temple now regretted his own grasping behavior. In reply to the monk's unspoken question, Tenzin nodded, then drew in a deep breath.

"I'll be fine."

His words were punctuated by a sudden blast: the monk turned in time to see the generator that powered Struker's evil machine exploding in a burst of shrapnel and smoke. The room was filled with crackles and bolts of electricity.

Making sure the others preceded him, the monk fled.

Along with all the others, including the rescued monks, Jade stumbled out into the lobby of the Human Rights Organization Building. Knowing what she knew now, it seemed even eerier than it had the first time she'd stood inside it.

Yet this time she felt no chill: She knew the evil had been conquered, and she had never been happier, because Kar and the monk were with her. She knew, too, that she had fulfilled at least one important part of her destiny, and the sense of triumph was heady.

So was the exhaustion. She passed by the towering statue of the dove bearing the olive branch—a beautiful symbol of peace—and it was there she allowed herself to do what the others had already done: collapse with a sigh against the cool floor. Until this moment, sheer tension had kept her going; now she realized the extreme exertion she'd put her body through, and the literal beating it had taken.

Kar was beside her. They hugged, sitting, while Fuktastic heartily congratulated his crew for getting out alive.

"It's over," Jade said happily.

"Not yet," the monk's voice countered. Jade looked up; the monk alone was still standing. Unlike the others, he had not allowed himself to sink to the floor to rest; instead, he stood alone, watching Jade and Kar intently. His face glowed with an almost paternal pride.

He stepped over to Kar and touched him gently on the shoulder. "You're the Next, Kar."

Kar stared up at him, slack-jawed, honestly confused. "What do you—?"

The nameless monk gestured to his Tibetan brothers. "When you freed them, you fulfilled the third prophecy: *He will lead the brothers he never knew to rejoin the family he never had.* It's the Year of the Ram again—the fifth complete cycle of the Chinese zodiac since the scroll passed into my care." He reached down and took Kar's hands. "My time has ended. Yours has come."

Moments before, Struker had come to and discovered his invention destroyed—and the magical power that had infused his body entirely gone. His youth, at least, remained . . . but his skull ached terribly, and his mouth tasted of blood. He raised the fingers of his uninjured hand to his head and lips and examined them: they were bright red with fresh blood.

He groaned as he pushed himself to his feet, and grabbed his side as he drew in a hitching breath; the sharp pain indicated broken ribs, a condition he had suffered many years ago—in Tibet.

For a moment, he stared in the darkness at his abandoned, crackling machine, and experienced the same anguish he had felt in 1945, when the war—and his glorious dream—had ended in defeat.

He could feel the youth beginning to leave his body . . . a familiar twinge of arthritis, one in his knee that he had not developed until his fifties, warned of the return of age.

So this was it, then: the monk had won. It would take years for Struker to re-create his machine—years he did not have. There was only one thing he *could* salvage from his sixty years of effort: revenge.

He moved slowly into the antechamber, and drew from his desk drawer the pistol there—the very Luger that he had worn to Tibet in 1943.

Staggering, he made his way up the stairs, toward the door that led to the main lobby. Before he arrived, he could hear voices . . . voices that filled him with an evil hope.

He stumbled out into the lobby, where the entire group of escapees sat facing him . . . and facing *them*, with his back turned to Struker—a perfect target—stood the monk.

With trembling hands, Struker lifted his pistol to eye level, aimed directly at the monk's back—right where the heart should be—and tightened his finger on the trigger.

"Time . . . to . . . *die* . . ." he whispered.

In the interim, Kar listened in awe and disbelief to the monk. He had known that he'd always been destined to rescue the monk, to have his life profoundly changed forever by the Tibetan. He knew, too, that his fate and Jade's were meant to be intertwined forever.

But Kar couldn't help feeling that the monk was simply mistaken about his being the Next. As honored and flattered as Kar felt, it simply didn't *feel* right, not the way that it had felt *so* right to him, setting off with Jade to rescue the monk and his brothers of the secret temple.

As he listened to the monk explain the third prophecy, Kar fancied he saw movement in the stairwell leading up to the lobby level. It had to be his imagination; Struker and his men were all out cold, and would be for a long time.

But then, as the monk leaned down to take Kar's hands in his, Kar saw the unthinkable: Struker, blood caked on his forehead and down the side of his face, stepping out into the lobby against the backdrop of bigger-than-life-sized photos of atrocities.

And in Struker's hands was a gleaming pistol. The Nazi aimed it directly at the monk.

Kar did not reflect, did not think, did not hesitate; his body moved on pure instinct.

"LOOK OUT!" he shouted.

Struker fired. The gunshot echoed through the vast, high-ceilinged lobby, startling everyone—all except Kar, who had already knocked the monk aside.

Yet there was no time for Kar to move out of the bullet's path himself. Time seemed to slow: he watched, amazed, as the bullet tore into his chest, as blood rushed out of the wound, rapidly staining his shirt a deep crimson.

He let go a gasp, half from surprise, half from a sudden desperate hunger for oxygen. The pain was stunning, worse than any blow he had ever sustained practicing martial arts, worse than he had ever imagined a bullet wound could feel: it felt as though his entire chest and all the bones and organs there had been utterly crushed; it felt as though they were all on fire.

Air rushed from Kar's lungs as he crumpled to his knees, vaguely aware that he was dying.

Jade watched in horror as Kar took the bullet intended for the monk. For an instant, she was far too stunned to move, to speak; instead, she merely stared at the monk as he immediately went to the stricken Kar's side.

For the brief time that Jade had known him, the monk's expression had almost always been one of calm acceptance, or of confident knowing mixed with good humor. Now the monk's eyes were filled with the purest despair. Jade rose and went over to them both . . . and fought back a rush of tears at the sight of Kar's wound.

He had been shot through the heart. He was gasping, pale with shock; his shirt was soaked with blood, and the stain was rapidly spreading.

"No . . ." Jade said.

Despite her desire not to believe it, the fact was, he was dying.

Jade wheeled about and charged Struker. He still held a gun in his trembling hand—and on his face was a look of deranged satisfaction. If he could not have the ultimate power, Jade realized, he would content himself with killing whoever he could, just to cause misery.

She rushed at him, not caring about the pistol pointed directly at her; she felt such utter conviction, such a sense of *rightness* that, at the moment, she felt capable of dodging even bullets. But she could not let him get away with even one more act of evil.

Struker aimed at Jade's skull, squeezed the trigger . . .

. . . and went wide-eyed with panic as the gun clicked harmlessly, out of ammunition.

Jade's righteous fury increased. "*Noooooooooo-ooooooooo!!!!!!!!!!!!!!*" she cried.

She met the Nazi head-on and, with a power that surprised her, launched into him with a spin-kick. The force of it sent Struker smashing into the base of the huge peace statue.

With the impact, the statue let out a low, metal groan.

The fallen Struker rolled his bloodied eyes upward and saw the dove of peace at the pinnacle begin to sway. Jade realized what was coming and moved out of the way . . . but the Nazi was not so agile or so fortunate. He tried to recover in time, tried to scramble away. . . .

With a giant creak, the heavy dove statue came

crashing down, directly on top of Struker. His body was covered beneath the rubble, invisible—but a single hand crept out from beneath it, spasmed for a few seconds, then went limp.

He was dead, Jade realized—and even though he had mortally wounded her dearest friend, she felt a sudden compassion for him, a sudden strange and overwhelming urge to pray that his spirit might be redeemed in a future life.

Then she turned all attention from Struker, and raced over to Kar. The monk looked at her sadly; unable to speak to him, she felt as though her heart had been torn in two.

She lifted Kar from the cold marble floor and cradled him in her arms. Despite all the blood, despite his alarming pallor, Kar's face was filled with a serene radiance; it was as though, Jade thought, she were looking at the monk.

Kar smiled weakly up at her, his expression one of pure joy. "Hey, girl . . ."

"Oh God, Kar," Jade said. There was so much she wanted to say to him, yet she seemed to have no other words. "Oh, God . . ." She looked over at the monk. "I don't understand. You said he was the Next, you said—"

The monk forced himself to regain his composure, and his confidence. "He *is*." He took Kar's hand. "Concentrate, Kar. Hold on. . . ."

The monk's body began to emanate a golden, glittering aura. . . . *Power*, Jade thought, awestruck by what she was witnessing. She could sense the pure energy. And just as she had known and sensed the Evil emanating from Struker's grand-daughter, now she could sense the Supreme Good.

Impossibly, the tattoos on the monk's flesh began to swirl and move, like living entities. Jade watched, dumbstruck, as they traveled, along with the glowing energy, down the monk's arm as if it were a conduit . . .

. . . and onto Kar's flesh.

I'm witnessing a true miracle, Jade realized. And in that instant, she believed. Believed utterly in everything her old Tibetan language instructor had told her about the reality of enlightenment and the buddhas who had achieved it, about death and re-birth and karma, about the power of compassion; believed utterly in the reality of the Next and the scroll.

And when she believed, her body began to tingle with power, with a sense of love, as if she were somehow connected to all the Enlightened Ones, as if they were gazing down on her, smiling with approval and everlasting affection.

Filled with that same love, Jade gazed down at Kar with hope . . .

. . . and saw, with the most profound sense of surprise she had ever known, the tattoos moving across Kar's flesh, and onto her own.

15

The monk stared, thunderstruck, as the scroll passed from Kar's flesh onto Jade's. For an instant, he looked up at her in disbelief . . .

. . . then forced himself to recall all the prophecies his master had taught him.

He remembered Jade back at Mista Fuktastic's subway warehouse headquarters, slyly kicking Kar the long iron rod that allowed him to defend himself; and Jade, talking Fuktastic out of killing Kar.

He will defeat an army of enemies while a flock of cranes circle above . . .

The monk's memory traveled back to Jade at her father's mansion, trading blows with Kar.

He will battle for love in a palace of jade . . .

And he recalled Jade, helping to free the captive monks from Struker's infernal device.

And he will lead the brothers he never knew to rejoin the family he never had . . .

The monk looked into Jade's tear-filled eyes. "It was you," he said, as revelation dawned. "All the time. *It was you.*"

Jade's breath caught in her throat; she returned the monk's gaze with eyes filled with grief and confusion.

Kar smiled faintly up at her, then glanced at the monk. The life was fading from him rapidly now, leaving his voice very weak, so weak that the monk had to lean in to hear him.

"Hey, I figured it out . . . why hot dogs come in packages of ten but hot dog *buns* come in packages of only eight. You just have to accept that, no matter how hard you try, you can never, ever have everything you want . . . so be happy with what you've got—'cause you can always have a hot dog."

The monk smiled down at his student. "Knowing others means you're wise . . . but knowing yourself means . . ."

Kar smiled back as he finished the monk's sentence, his voice trailing to a whisper. ". . . you're enlightened."

The monk nodded, trying to hold back his human tears. There was no real need to grieve, he reminded himself; Kar had fulfilled his karma and achieved some measure of enlightenment. He would have a good rebirth, and the monk did not doubt that, in the next life, they would meet again.

Kar let go a hitching breath, then fell back limply.

Jade at once took his face in her hands. "Aw, no.

Kar? Kar . . ." And at the realization that he was gone, she began to weep openly.

As for the monk, he felt a sudden, distinct weakness. Instinct made him glance down at his hands—which were slowly starting to wrinkle as time began to make its mark.

He slowly rose, and watched as his body—free for the first time in sixty years of the sacred tattoos—began to sag and age, until it at last attained his true age of ninety years. He stood and studied the Next.

Jade looked up at last from her sorrow to find the monk now wizened with age, his hair the color of snow, but his eyes were the same: ageless and wise.

She knew that what had just occurred was supremely important—so important that she knew she had to put all her own personal concerns aside, even her grief over the loss of Kar. But mixed in with the sense of power and enlightenment she had earlier experienced was a small thread of fear. *How can I ever fulfill such a noble task? Certainly I'm not worthy. . . .*

But the scroll said otherwise; she knew she had no choice but to humbly accept her destiny.

She brushed away her tears.

"Are you ready?" the monk asked, his voice now thin and reedy.

Jade met his gaze and nodded firmly. "One . . . complete . . . life."

For the first time, she noticed that the monks had risen from their place and now faced her in a semicircle. As she looked askance at them, they bowed low to her, a gesture of respect.

In the distance, police sirens began to wail. It was time for them to leave, Jade realized.

She permitted herself one long, last look at Kar's lifeless body—then, on impulse, she leaned down and gently kissed him.

Sparks of energy flew where their lips met; a surge of power flowed through Jade's body, and she opened her eyes, dazzled by a sudden brilliant, white light. . . .

A few weeks later, the monk stood at the waterfront, preparing to board the large freighter that would carry him to Nepal, now a refuge for most of the Tibetans displaced by the Chinese invasion.

He smiled at the Next, she who had been known as Jade, now the Sister With No Name. She had responded quite amazingly with only a short period of training, and the old monk could now leave her with pride and total confidence in her abilities.

"Your training is complete," he told her. "Now . . ."

He leaned forward, his lips close to her ear. "The last verse of the scroll . . ." He whispered it to her, then drew back and kissed her affectionately on the forehead.

To his amazement, a small, brightly colored butterfly fluttered through the air between them and settled atop the nameless sister's head. She raised a hand to her hair, tenderly prodded the creature into her palm, then held it before her and carefully stroked its wings.

She who was once called Jade smiled over at her aged master, and uttered words she had no doubt heard somewhere before . . . perhaps, the monk thought, in a past life, atop a Himalayan mountain six decades ago. "Enjoy your vacation . . . Master."

And she released a gentle breath on the butterfly's back. It flew off in the direction of the setting sun; the monk watched it go with a sense of fulfillment. His duty on this earth had been accomplished: all was as it should be.

A familiar voice interrupted them with feigned annoyance. "Are you two through?"

The Sister With No Name turned and directed a playful grin at Kar, then gestured with her chin at the monk. "He's all yours."

The monk watched with a welling of affection as Kar faced him, his expression suddenly awkward. After a time, Kar said, "Look . . . I just want to say . . . well—"

The monk smiled tenderly at his young friend. "No words are necessary. I feel the same way."

Kar hesitated—then, unable to contain himself any longer, he lurched forward and gave the monk a huge hug.

They separated reluctantly . . . and the monk, to lighten Kar's pain, promptly checked his pockets.

Kar frowned faintly, puzzled. "What are you doing?"

"Checking to see that nothing's missing," the monk retorted. "I remember the *first hug* you gave me."

They exchanged a grin.

The monk pulled out a locket from his jacket. The glass had been shattered by Nina Struker's heel, but it was removed now, and the undamaged daguerreotype of Amra of Gyangze remained. To his utter joy, he had learned, with the help of the brothers of a temple in Nepal, that Amra still lived. And now she waited for him. Truly, the buddhas had repaid him well for his life of service.

He snapped the locket shut and allowed himself a last, affectionate glance at his worthy successors.

Then, without clinging, without grasping any further to his former life, the monk turned and walked up the gangplank to the ship, to his new existence.

She who used to be Jade climbed onto her motorcycle, parked at the side of the dock, then waited for Kar to seat himself behind her. Once he was settled, she gave him a little shit.

"You know, you still haven't thanked me for kissing your ass back to life."

Behind her, Kar shook his head. "Man, I'm not sure which is worse: death—or being the sidekick to a hot babe who's taken a Solemn Vow of Abstinence."

The nameless sister flashed him a wry smile. "Tell me about it."

She hit the gas; the bike lurched, causing Kar to tighten his hold around her midsection, and she smiled again, this time to herself. She was, she knew, at last experiencing one complete life, a *genuine* one instead of two false ones, and she was prepared for the task that lay ahead, even one that might require sixty years. She had not only Kar to help her, but the support of all the brothers of the secret temple—as well as the wisdom of her master, which would remain forever in her mind and heart.

By the time they had made their way back into the center of the city, the Sister With No Name noticed something in the motorcycle's rearview mirror: first one black sedan following them . . . then two, then three, then four.

For a time, she managed to outpace them. And then the first black sedan revved its engine and approached at top speed, close enough for her to recognize the driver peering through the windshield.

It was Nina Struker, still alive, still relentlessly pursuing her grandfather's dream of total power.

She who used to be Jade swerved the bike around in a one-eighty, and skidded to a halt. Time for a face-off. She could sense Kar's total trust in her decision: his hands around her waist didn't tighten even a millimeter, but remained loose and relaxed.

She watched as Nina's hand appeared out of the driver's-side window, clutching a gun. Without hesitation, the blond woman aimed and fired directly at the nameless sister.

But the former Jade's training was complete, as her master had said. She dodged the impossible-to-dodge bullet with ease, then flashed a quick smile back at Kar. "Hold on tight."

She gunned the bike and charged straight off the oncoming sedans, zooming off a ramp and flying atop the bike into the air. . . .

And at that moment, she felt no fear, no worry, no concern, only a sense of fulfillment. For she knew that she and Kar would be successful, whether she chose to escape her pursuers this day or to battle them directly. The scroll would be safe.

And her mission with Kar was only beginning. . . .